THE DONKEY'S GIFT

Books by Thomas M. Coffey

AGONY AT EASTER

IMPERIAL TRAGEDY

LION BY THE TAIL

THE LONG THIRST: PROHIBITION IN AMERICA

DECISION OVER SCHWEINFURT

HAP: A BIOGRAPHY OF GENERAL HENRY H. ARNOLD

THE DONKEY'S GIFT

Thomas M. Coffey

ILLUSTRATIONS BY
HAL JUST

CROWN PUBLISHERS, INC.
NEW YORK

Published by Crown Publishers, Inc.,
One Park Avenue, New York, New York 10016, and
simultaneously in Canada by
General Publishing Company Limited
Manufactured in the United States of America
Library of Congress Cataloging in Publication Data
Coffey, Thomas M.
The donkey's gift.
Summary: A strong, rebellious donkey with a checkered career is sold
to a man named Joseph, and during a journey to Bethlehem proves a
great help to him and his pregnant wife Mary.
1. Donkeys—Fiction.   2. Mary, Blessed Virgin, Saint—Fiction.
3. Christmas stories.   [1. Christmas—Fiction.   2. Donkeys—
Fiction]   I. Title.
PS3553.0364D6   1984   813'.54 [Fic]   84-199
ISBN 0-517-55414-3
10 9 8 7 6 5 4 3 2 1
First Edition

Designed by Shari deMiskey

THE DONKEY'S GIFT

CHAPTER ONE

GAIN ASINUS HAD GOT HIMSELF INTO AN apparently hopeless mess. Though he was known among his kind as the biggest, strongest, proudest donkey in all Palestine, here he was on the block once more, subject to the kicks and blows of still another mean and foulmouthed dealer; and this time in the filthiest donkey yard he had ever seen, at the edge of the scruffiest town he had ever seen. But when a donkey refused to carry a load, he had to be ready to bear a cruel burden. A rebel's life was never easy.

The man who now possessed him—a huge, grimy, round-bellied scoundrel named Ezekiel—was undoubtedly the worst of the many dealers through whose hands Asinus had passed. Ezekiel never spent a shekel to shelter the beasts he bought and sold. When night came they huddled together for warmth at the bottom of the rough, sloping yard. But Ezekiel had spent enough money for a stout fence to keep them from escaping. The water in their trough was seldom clean, and much of the feed he bought for them, at bargain prices, had been stored so long it was fermenting. This rancid feed had caused, indirectly, Asinus's first difficulty with Ezekiel.

The day after the dealer bought him, Asinus had overheard a prospective customer speak up about the hay in the feed bin: "It smells like rotten wine," the man exclaimed. "Don't tell me you give this to your donkeys?"

Ezekiel, who had lost so many front teeth he spoke with a lisp, said, "Why not? They're too thtupid to know the differenth."

Asinus, always quick to anger at the charge that donkeys were stupid, swung around and aimed both rear hooves at Ezekiel's plump behind, propelling him into the air, then onto his fat belly in the middle of a squishy mud puddle. Ezekiel had not taken kindly to the experience. After wiping the mire from his face, he had come at Asinus with a stout stave and with several impolite epithets. Before he was through, he seemed to have had the last word on the stupidity of donkeys. He had, at least, convinced the other donkeys.

"That should teach you," one of them said to Asinus. "You can't argue with staves."

But Asinus had been neither convinced nor intimidated. "I can still outwit a donkey skinner," he insisted. "And so could all of us. If we refused to work, they'd turn us loose."

"They haven't turned you loose," another donkey observed cynically.

Though this conversation took place in front of Ezekiel, he was oblivious of it. Like most people, he didn't know donkeys could talk to each other.

"I can't see why you have so much respect for people," Asinus said to the other donkeys. "Look how they use us. The fact is, we donkeys are splendid creatures. Any one of us can carry more than a horse, on half as much hay. Yet you see how people pamper their horses. They even treat dogs better than donkeys. If we had any self-respect, we'd all revolt."

"How?" asked an old, swaybacked roan. "I, too, used to think I could outwit people, but I found out they were too smart."

"If men are so smart," Asinus insisted, "how come we can understand every order we get from this vicious bully, but he can't understand a word we say?"

"And if donkeys are so smart," the old roan asked, "how come we spend our lives penned up like this, while men walk free?"

"It has nothing to do with brains," Asinus argued. "It's only because an accident of nature gave them hands and gave us hooves. If I had hands so I could go after Ezekiel with staves, how long would he last against me?"

Two days later, a little jenny, who had been eyeing Asinus, came to him with alarming news. She had heard Ezekiel say he intended to have Asinus slaughtered for horsemeat.

Though this sounded unlikely, Asinus could not discount it. Besides being an amazingly large donkey, he had amazingly small ears. He could almost pass for a horse, if he weren't so proud to be a donkey. Because of his size and apparent strength, dealers had always been able to find buyers for him. Everyone assumed he could carry a heavier load than other donkeys, and indeed he could. What buyers were never told was that he refused to do so. They discovered that when they tried to put packs on his back.

The next day, Ezekiel brought in a buyer who closely examined the big gray-white donkey, but not the way a driver would examine him. This man was more interested in the size of Asinus's rump than the strength of his back. And Ezekiel, instead of describing him as "strong" and "surefooted," was using words like "tender" and "delicious."

It was the ultimate insult, the ultimate proof of man's inhumanity to donkeys and of everything Asinus had been saying about men. But he had no time to take satisfaction in that. His life was at stake. He had to flee, and quickly. He knew where to go—into the highest hills of Galilee, where a donkey could forage for himself with dignity, away from cruel, exploitative, murderous mankind. But first he would have to escape from this cruelest of men, Ezekiel, the donkey dealer.

Fortunately for Asinus, the other donkeys in the yard sympathized with him. Though they didn't think he was very bright when he challenged the ascendancy of man, they nevertheless admired him for it. And they were appalled at his apparent fate. The possibility of a donkey ending up as horsemeat is repugnant to all donkeys. They agreed to help him escape. But they didn't know how.

Asinus was full of ideas. There is nothing like the imminent danger of death for inspiring ideas. He wondered if he would be able to burrow under the fence. After all, donkeys were sometimes called burros. In their remote past, they must have been able to dig. Yet Asinus felt he had no talent for it.

He thought first of getting a good run from the top of the yard and jumping the fence at the bottom. Everyone said he looked like a horse, and horses were notorious jumpers. A man had only to show a whip to a horse and the silly creature would leap over a fence, a wall, a hedge, or any other impossible obstacle he might find in front of him. But Asinus didn't know how high he could jump. It took practice, even for horses, to develop a talent for high jumping. And once they mastered it, there was little use for it. After a high jump, there was nothing to do but to come back down. On the other hand, if you leaped straight ahead, it could get you across a chasm or a river. Donkeys were well known for their ability to leap straight ahead. Further evidence of their good sense. He'd like to be able to jump over the fence at the bottom of the yard, but what would the other donkeys think? They'd accuse him of making a horse of himself.

He'd have to come up with something safer and simpler. Finally he worked out a scheme so appealing to the other donkeys that they all fell in with it eagerly. The very next day, they would try it.

Dawn came dark, cold and rainy, ideal for an escaping donkey inasmuch as it would be no fun for people to chase him through the wet, unpaved, dreary streets of Nazareth, but not so ideal for launching the escape, since it depended upon the arrival of customers at the donkey yard. It was midmorning before the first customer arrived. As soon as Ezekiel opened the gate to let him in, the old roan, who had belittled Asinus's campaign against men, nevertheless stepped forward to play the key role in Asinus's bid for freedom. The roan was such an aged, docile donkey, the mule dealer allowed him to wander unwatched. This time, while Ezekiel was wringing his hands and smiling effusively at the prospective buyer, the roan wandered to the partly opened gate and, with a nudge of his shoulder, flung it wide open.

The moment of opportunity had arrived. Every donkey in the yard rushed toward the gate and stampeded through it, as if bent on freedom.

Ezekiel, preceded by his prodigious belly, waddled after them, shouting, "Come back, you mitherable creaturth!"

But he apparently didn't expect them to comply, because when they stopped, turned and came stampeding obediently back toward him, his face became a mask of consternation. Skidding in the mud, he lost his balance and once more landed in a puddle, this time on the seat of his toga.

The sight of Ezekiel helpless on the ground in front of them created a temptation for the donkeys. Every one of them had reason to trample him, but it was not part of their plan. Displaying the admirable single-mindedness for which donkeys are famous, they slowed their stampede, giving him time to scramble frantically to his feet. Dripping mud from his rear, he ran for his life back into the yard with all of his donkeys at his heels, nudging him along. That is to say, all but one of his donkeys. Asinus, of course, had continued on, as planned, when the others turned back.

By the time Ezekiel got hold of a stave thick enough to restore order, Asinus was running up one of the steep streets of the hilly town. The donkey dealer, counting heads, soon discovered that one donkey was missing and realized which one it was.

"Aha! I might have known!" he exclaimed as he looked up the hill and caught a glimpse of the high-tailing Asinus. Moments later, the infuriated dealer was aboard the biggest, strongest donkey left to him, ascending the street in pursuit. But not with the speed he needed. His mount, having just taken part in the effort to free Asinus, was hardly eager to help capture him. Instead of running up the hill, he followed a halting, wayward course, earning for himself a series of blows sharp enough to influence him mightily under ordinary circumstances, but hardly even noticeable to him in the midst of all this excitement. At last, under the rain of blows, the donkey did finally begin to run at top speed, but not to catch Asinus. Ahead, at the opening of a narrow street, was a vegetable peddler's stall. The galloping donkey, despite Ezekiel's best efforts to control him, raced directly toward this stall, then, a few feet from it, practiced another skill for which donkeys are famous—the technique of sudden stops. Since humans are much less adept at sudden stops than donkeys, Ezekiel continued at top speed, right onto the pile of vegetables.

The peddler was vexed at this until Ezekiel explained that it was the fault of a runaway donkey. It seems that if a man wants sympathy from another man, he has only to blame his troubles on a donkey. The peddler soon began telling Ezekiel about a donkey he once had, which was the most stubborn in all Galilee, but Ezekiel at the moment didn't need any new donkey stories. Tethering his recalcitrant mount, he ran up the street on foot after Asinus.

It was beginning to look now as if Asinus, racing through the wet, sparsely peopled streets of Nazareth, might make good his escape. He had built up a sizable lead on Ezekiel, and he was much faster afoot. But as he began savoring his freedom, the rain stopped, the clouds parted, the warm sun shone down and Nazarenes by the hundreds began pouring out of their houses. Ezekiel's "Runaway donkey!" cries, catching their attention, seemed to exhilarate them. Chasing runaway donkeys had always been a favorite sport. Let a dangerous criminal get loose in the street and people would flee into their houses, bolting the doors and windows. But let a harmless donkey get loose and they'd all come out, hoping to grab his tail and give it a tug.

Asinus now saw, in the street ahead of him, a gang of ragged urchins, waving their arms to stop him. He avoided them by turning right, into a trash-filled alley, but when he emerged into the next street, he confronted a whole swarm of people running toward him. He broke through this motley crowd at full speed, but as he ran into a crooked little street with a dozen jabbering men behind him, he found another dozen in front of him. He was trapped for sure this time. Or was he? At the most opportune moment, a woman, attracted by the commotion, emerged from her house and left the front door open. Asinus, veering to the left, ran into the house, past a child asleep in a crib and a startled old man who was lifting a piece of bread to his mouth, then out the back door into another alley that led to another street.

Up and down the hilly streets of Nazareth the desperate chase continued until Asinus spotted a herd of donkeys in an open field near the edge of town. Without so much as a by-your-leave, he joined them, hoping to lose himself among them. But he had just begun to graze nonchalantly in their midst, lowering his head to prevent his inordinately large size from giving him away, when their owner came along and began herding them together.

"What does he want?" Asinus asked the donkey nearest him.

"We're traveling with a caravan to Magdala," the other donkey said. "Why don't you come along? We could use a big donkey like you. Lighten the loads for the rest of us."

"No thank you," Asinus said. "I've never been able to see myself with a pack on my back. Where does it get you?" Warming to his subject, he launched into the same set speech he had delivered to so many other donkeys. But alas, these were no more disposed to listen to him than the others. Slowly they drifted away at the heels of their owner and Asinus found himself alone in the field, exposed once more to the crowds of Nazarenes looking for him.

As soon as they spotted him they were after him again, but now Asinus was tired and discouraged. Despite a series of adroit turns and dodges that preserved his freedom for another half hour or so, he finally stumbled into what proved to be a cul-de-sac. The howling mob was quickly upon him, swarming all over him, pulling his tail, knocking him about, entangling his legs and neck in heavy ropes. Bone-weary, dripping perspiration and gasping for air, he leaned against a rough stone wall, almost oblivious of the pummeling hands on his body. But he anticipated with fear and dejection the moment when the furious Ezekiel would come to reclaim him.

CHAPTER TWO

ETHERED SECURELY TO A POST, ASINUS pranced from foot to foot as the cursing and accursed Ezekiel belabored his flanks with a long, thick cudgel. The unfortunate donkey, a connoisseur of drubbings, decided this was the worst he had ever absorbed during a lifetime of defiance against mankind. Ezekiel seemed determined to leave no part unbruised. His rage was so intense and his attack so vigorous that the possibility of his exhausting himself seemed the only hope for the donkey's survival. The beating had been in progress for some time and, indeed, the dealer was showing signs of overexertion, when he was interrupted by the arrival of a tall, slender man with an adz dangling from his belt. Obviously a carpenter.

Standing at the gate, the man called out to Ezekiel: "Sir! I beg you, sir, not to beat that donkey!"

Ezekiel paused just long enough to bellow in reply: "I'm not beating him. I'm tenderithing him before I thell him to a butcher!" With that, he gave Asinus three more resounding whacks.

"But why, sir? Why?" the carpenter cried. "What could he have done?"

"What could he have done?" Ezekiel's indignation showed in his face. "He tore up the town. Who do you think hath to pay for that?"

Nazareth was still abuzz with the story of the big donkey chase. Some people were proclaiming it the longest chase on record. Many compared it favorably to a famous chase in Cana twenty-seven years earlier, in which a dozen runaway donkeys sprinted through the streets and seven people were injured. Admittedly, no one was injured in the chase after Asinus, but he had easily broken all records for damage to shops and merchandise.

"Is this the donkey that tried to run away?" the carpenter asked.

"None other," said Ezekiel, landing another blow.

"I pray you, sir, let me in. I must get a closer look at him."

Ezekiel not only opened the gate for the carpenter, he offered him his cudgel. "Here, you pound on him for a while," he said. "I'm a bit arm-weary. Not tho young anymore."

The carpenter, after drawing back momentarily from the cudgel, then took it from Ezekiel. Asinus prepared himself for a fresh onslaught. He expected now that he would be beaten to death. By the time this fellow finished, the word would be around town and people would line up to take turns on him. But to his surprise, the carpenter, even before approaching him, threw the cudgel over the fence. Instead of punching him, the man gently patted his head.

"Looks like a strong creature," he said to Ezekiel. "And big! I don't think I've ever seen a donkey this big."

"I'm glad of that," said Ezekiel, "becauth I'm thelling him by the pound."

"You're not serious! My dear man, he's a prize specimen. And he's in his prime. I'll bet he can carry an enormous load."

Asinus, amazed and relieved at first by the carpenter's gentle gesture, was now able to see through his game. What the man really wanted was the same thing all men wanted from donkeys. To pile heavy loads on their backs.

It was a measure of Ezekiel's fury against Asinus that even the possibility of selling him for a profit did not shake his resolve to send him to a slaughterhouse. He was so enraged at the animal, he was willing—uncharacteristically—even to take a loss for the satisfaction of seeing him dead.

"My friend," he said to the carpenter, "I got the

betht donkeyth in town. Look at them over there. Friendly, dependable, hardworking. Every one of them can carry a load. And believe you me, they're prithed to thell. Go pick one out. Take it for a little trot around the block. I'll give you a bargain you can't match."

"But what if I don't want any of those?" the carpenter asked. "What if I want this one?"

Ezekiel flashed a toothless smile and put his arm on the man's shoulder. "Lithen," he said, "I couldn't live with mythelf if I thold him to you. I got a reputation. I treat people right. I wouldn't even thell that demon to a Roman general."

"You mean, just because he ran away?"

"Becauth he ran away!" Ezekiel exclaimed. "Running away ith only the beginning. He'th mean, ornery, lathy, wild, wicked, pigheaded, contrary and thtubborn. You put all that together in one donkey, you ain't got a donkey. You got a catathtrophe. You lay a load on hith back, he'll throw it off. You tell him to go, he'll thtand. I tried everything with that devil. You'll never know how good I treated him. I gave him new-mown hay. I gave him honey. But would he do a thing I told him to do?"

"Maybe if you were more gentle with him . . ." the carpenter suggested.

"Gentle! You want gentle! Go ahead. Be gentle with him. Then get up on his back. I dare you."

"It's hard to believe he can be that bad," the carpenter said. "Animals are like people. Treat them well and they'll treat you well."

Asinus, listening to the man, wondered if he could be as trusting as he sounded. When you invite a brigand into your home, will he not rob you anyway? When you pet a lion, will he not eat you? Asinus had learned about nature, human and animal, on the streets, where he had spent his life. He had never encountered, among the crooks, soldiers, bandits, donkey drivers, peddlers and unscrupulous merchants who had owned him, anyone who believed in such golden rules. If this man actually lived by what he said, he might prove useful. Asinus knew now that if he didn't get away from Ezekiel, he was doomed. And escape would not be easy. The morning's failure proved that. But if he could ingratiate himself with this carpenter, if he could turn on so much donkey charm that the fellow would insist on having him, and keep offering more money for him until Ezekiel's greed finally overcame his anger, then at least the fatal trip to the butcher's shop would be averted.

Asinus was not the only one bemused by the carpenter's gullibility. Ezekiel stared with mouth agape, as if he were seeing someone from another world. "If you think you can get that animal to treat you well," he invited, "be my guetht. Untie him. Try to ride him."

The carpenter walked over to Asinus and patted him gently once more. "What's his name?" he asked. "Does he have a name?"

"The dirty crook who thold him to me called him Athinuth. I call him Beelthebub."

The carpenter extended his callused hands and

began to untie the donkey. "Stand still, Asinus. That's a good fellow."

Ezekiel retreated to a safe distance. "Remember," he warned, "it'th your fault if you get hurt."

As the ropes fell away, Asinus pulled himself up to his full height, stretching his battered flesh. With a slow turn of his head, he rubbed his muzzle against the man's shoulder. The gesture seemed to work. The man smiled. "You see," he said to Ezekiel, "he's not so wild."

"Wait till you try to mount him."

The carpenter hoisted himself onto Asinus, whose first impulse was to jettison him summarily as he had done to so many other men. The weight of a man on his back offended his dignity. But today he must accept it if he wanted to be alive tomorrow. Suppressing his indignation, he stood still while the man made himself comfortable. Then at the man's command, he walked painfully around the yard.

"I can't believe it," Ezekiel exclaimed. "That beating did him a lot of good."

"Are you sure it was the beating?"

"What elth?"

"I think he's a marvelous beast," the carpenter said, dismounting. "I really would like to buy him."

Ezekiel gave the man a long, appraising look. "After what I thaid about him?"

"Well, I'm sorry you had trouble with him, but I want him. I've never seen his equal."

Ezekiel, with a curious look on his face, continued to study the carpenter. Finally he broke into an egregious smile and said, "You know a donkey when you thee one, don't you?"

"It's easy to see that this one is exceptional," the carpenter said.

Ezekiel nodded. "Right you are, mithter. No finer donkey in all Galilee. Couldn't fool you about that, could I? Maybe I ought to thell him to you. But can you afford him?"

"I don't know, sir. How much do you want?"

Ezekiel again looked the man over carefully. "Twelve shekelth."

When Asinus heard this his hopes fell. Nobody paid that much for a donkey. But to his amazement, the man stared upward as if counting his money in his mind, then said, "All right, I'll take him."

Asinus was flabbergasted. The poor fellow hadn't even tried to bargain. It was embarrassing to be sold to someone so easily duped. On the other hand, what difference did it make? Asinus intended to stay with him only long enough to arrange an escape. And that should be easy.

Asinus now took his first close look at his new owner and decided that, for a human being, he was passable. He was hardly handsome, but neither was he ugly. His features, though blunt, were quite regular; his nose was wide, his mouth ample, his eyes pale green and so large he seemed at all times to be staring in wonder at the world around him. His gray hair, parted in the middle, fell almost to his neck in waves luxuriantly thick despite his age, which appeared to be about forty. Tall and muscular but still lean, he

showed not even the suggestion of a middle-aged paunch beneath his carpenter's apron.

After producing a large leather pouch from a pocket hidden in the folds of his garment, he loosened the drawstring and extracted a great handful of silver shekels. Then he counted out twelve, gave them to Ezekiel and thanked him for his courtesy. Returning his purse to its concealed pocket, he smiled at the huge gray-white donkey he had purchased and said to him, almost as if they were old friends or brothers, "Come on, Asinus, let's go home."

Ezekiel said, "I can give you a bridle. Even a thaddle if you want it, but they're both ecthtra."

The carpenter said, "We don't need anything like that, do we, Asinus?" Walking toward the gate, he glanced back at the donkey. "Come along."

Asinus had first to recover from his amazement at the man's colossal presumption. Then, in a daze, he, too, started toward the gate.

Ezekiel, watching the man walk away with the now-docile donkey at his heels, shook his head and blinked his eyes. "One of uth," he muttered, "ith even dumber than that infernal ath."

CHAPTER THREE

OLLOWING BEHIND HIS NEW OWNER, Asinus was so astonished to be unrestrained that they had walked almost a block before it occurred to him he could now make another bolt for freedom. And why should this fellow assume he wouldn't do so? Only two hours earlier he had turned the town upside down in his attempt to escape Ezekiel. But was this the moment to run for it again? What if a second attempt failed and the man returned him to Ezekiel? Perhaps he'd better wait awhile, find out more about the fellow, then choose the right time to escape.

The carpenter turned and said, "Do you see how many people keep staring at you? You're a handsome donkey, Asinus. I'd have gladly paid twice as much for you."

What that meant, Asinus decided, was that the man didn't know much about the price of donkeys. But he apparently knew something about carpentry. He looked prosperous and he had a heavy purseful of silver concealed in his garments. Too much, in fact, to carry in public, with so many thieves abroad.

It was midday now, and Nazareth was full of people shopping, hawking wares or simply enjoying the early winter sun. Scores of other donkeys kept passing him in the narrow streets, some led by merchants or peddlers and heavily laden with goods, others led by women and carrying nothing but bunches of twigs gathered for cooking. Was this how his new owner intended to use him? Being a carpenter, perhaps he needed a donkey to carry logs or planks. He could forget that. Lumber was heavy. Twigs wouldn't exactly be backbreaking, but they would be humiliating. Asinus refused to see himself being led through the streets by this man's wife, with a load of sticks on his back. Did the man have a wife? What would she be like? Probably old and ugly, with a foul disposition and a loud mouth.

As they passed the market area, the carpenter was accosted by a woman in rags. Asinus knew her immediately for what she was—a professional beggar. In

her darting eyes he saw no distress, but shrewd calcu-
lation. She blocked the carpenter's path by bowing
obsequiously before him.

"With such a donkey you must be a wealthy man,"
she said, ignoring the fact that he was dressed like a
carpenter. "Couldn't you spare just a shekel for my
poor, starving children?"

"How many children do you have?" he asked.

"Six little darlings, and they'd be here with me but
they're too weak to walk. I beg you, have mercy on
them."

Taking out his purse, he said, "My dear woman,
you can't feed six children with one shekel. Here's two
shekels for you. Go in peace."

Asinus, watching this transaction, was embarrassed
for the man. On the other hand, it was useful to know
he was so gullible. As they approached the neighborhood in which tradesmen lived, he noticed that the
houses they passed, while small, were better kept.
Even the streets were cleaner. Cooking smells wafted
through the open windows and voices echoed off the
stone walls. Children, neatly dressed in coarse garments, were playing in the streets. One of them pulled
Asinus's tail as he passed. Asinus kicked out wildly, as
a warning. He had never liked children. All they ever
wanted to do with donkeys was to ride them, whip
them, chase them, scream at them or pull their tails.
It seemed to him that boys and girls were simply min-
iature men and women, just as mean and just as de-
manding, but with shriller voices. The donkey had not
yet been born who could outbray a shrieking child.

They came eventually upon a long row of artisans'
workshops, open to the street, with small, attached
living quarters, some of brick, some of rough-hewn
stone, set into the hillside behind them. At one of
these shops the carpenter stopped. "Here we are," he
said to Asinus. "Your new home. Wait till my wife sees
you."

With that he trotted through his shop shouting,
"Mary! Mary! Come see what I've brought you!"

Asinus, left unattended at the entrance to the shop,
looked in at the piles of planks, the workbenches and
sawhorses, a half-finished table, an array of tools
hanging from nails on the far wall. It was a typical
carpenter's shop, with sawdust and shavings on the
floor and the sweet smell of lumber filling the air.

The carpenter emerged from his house pulling with
him a young woman—actually she looked more like a
teenaged girl—dressed in a long blue gown with a
dun-colored apron over it. She was wiping her hands
on the apron as her husband hurried her forth.

"Asinus, this is my wife, Mary," the carpenter said.
"Is she not the most beautiful woman in all Galilee?
Nay, in all the world?"

Asinus, staring at her transfixed, decided he could
believe that. Never before had he seen such a woman.
Always quick and eager to spot flaws in human beings,
he tried in vain to find any in her. She moved with
amazing grace, even as her husband dragged her by
the arm. Her great halo of thick black hair, the black-
est imaginable, framed a radiant face with the clear-
est, smoothest olive complexion imaginable. Her

mouth was smiling but her eyes—large, dark and wide open—looked a bit apprehensive, as if she were asking herself, What has this husband of mine done now? At second glance, Asinus noticed something else about her. She was great with child. Her time to deliver must be very nearly upon her. How did this middle-aged carpenter ever find so magnificent a wife?

"And are you not," the man continued, addressing Asinus, "the one donkey in all the world worthy to carry her?" Turning to his wife, he said, "Speak, my darling. How do you like him?"

When she walked up to Asinus and touched the side of his head, running her fingers along his cheek, it was hard for him to accept the notion that so light a touch could instill so warm a feeling. "He's beautiful," she said. "But how can we afford such a splendid donkey? Tell me, Joseph, where did you get him? How much did you pay for him?"

"Twelve, no, fourteen shekels," he said.

She looked incredulous. "Fourteen shekels for a donkey! You've been giving money away again, haven't you?"

"Well, just a little," he admitted sheepishly, "but what could I do? I came upon this starving woman who had six starving children."

"Did you see the children?"

"No, of course not. They were at home, all of them sick from lack of food."

"Do you mean to say you gave her six shekels?"

"Not at all. I gave her only two."

"But even that, my dear, is a lot of money. You

can't afford to help everyone you see. If you don't stop giving your money away, you won't have enough left to pay your taxes."

"Don't worry," he said, "God will provide."

To Asinus this seemed a ludicrous conversation. If the man really believed God was that good about providing, how would he explain why God hadn't provided for the supposedly starving woman and her six starving children? But maybe God had provided for her, by sending her this easy mark. And what was all this talk about paying taxes? Not one of the dozen or so men who had previously owned Asinus had ever paid taxes.

"If you gave the woman just two shekels," Mary continued, "where did the rest of the money go? You said fourteen. You didn't pay twelve for a donkey."

Asinus felt insulted by this remark. He couldn't deny that, at the market price for donkeys, she was right. Her husband had paid far too much for him. But why should the market price be so low? Why did humans have such small regard for donkeys? This woman, though undeniably beautiful, was just as insensitive to donkeys, he decided, as all the other people he had known.

"But, darling," her husband said, "can't you see what a marvelous donkey he is?"

"Even so, twelve shekels? Did you bargain with the man? No, I'll bet you took the first price he mentioned."

Joseph looked almost impatient. "Mary, you know how I hate it when someone bargains with me for my work. Why should I bargain with others? I'm sure the price was fair."

She shook her head, then suddenly changing her mood, smiled and kissed him. "All right, dear, if you're convinced. And he is a marvelous donkey. Just the same, do you think he'll be equal to such a load on such a long journey?"

"Have no fear of it," Joseph assured her. "He's the strongest donkey I've ever seen."

At the word *journey*, Asinus raised his ears. Was that why they had bought him? To use him as pack animal on some trip they were planning? They were out of their minds if they thought he'd carry their baggage for them even as far as the town limits. On the other hand, it would be one way to get out of this miserable town.

Joseph, perhaps to forestall any further questioning, said, "I must take the poor creature back and feed him. I'm sure he's hungry and tired."

Mary looked quizzical. "Tired? You just bought him. How could he get tired walking across town?"

"Well, you see, this morning he ran away from the man who owned him."

"Aha!" she exclaimed. "So this is the donkey everyone's talking about. And you paid twelve whole shekels for him?"

"I paid it gladly. He's no ordinary donkey."

"I hope not. But if he ran away from another man, why shouldn't he run away from you?"

"Because I'll treat him better. You should have seen the way that man was beating the unfortunate beast."

"So you bought him, then, to save him from a beating." Mary smiled, not with mockery but with warmth. Standing on tiptoes, she kissed her husband's chin. "Joseph, I have to love you when you do things like that. But I'll never know how you've managed to get safely through life."

With that she turned, petted Asinus again and went back into the house. Joseph led Asinus up a narrow passageway along the side of the building to a covered but otherwise open stall in the rear, which looked as if another donkey had once occupied it. "Here's a trough of fresh water for you," Joseph said. "And I'll mix a bit of grain with your hay. You'll be nice and comfortable. We used to have a little jenny, and she liked it here, I think, but she was just too small."

So you got rid of her, Asinus said to himself. Is that what you mean by treating me better? You'll give me fresh water and grain mixed with my hay as long as I'm big enough and willing to carry your loads. You don't fool me, Mr. Joseph. Some men control their donkeys by beatings. Others control us by pretending to be good to us. But all men get rid of us when we're no longer useful to them.

As soon as Asinus had eaten his fill, he was subjected to another of Joseph's insidious attempts to win his friendship. First came a thorough cleaning and currying. Then the carpenter, with his strong fingers, rubbed a soothing ointment into the donkey's battered flesh. For a few minutes, the pain seemed to increase, but gradually the balsam unguent took effect and Asinus could no longer deny that the treatment was doing him some good. Perversely, he almost wished it weren't so. He hated the thought of owing this man any gratitude.

As the wintery afternoon progressed, the temperature dropped, despite the sunshine, until, by nightfall, the air was frigid and a rising wind sharpened its bite. Asinus, huddling into the bed of straw in his stall, almost wished he were back among the donkeys on Ezekiel's lot. They, at least, had one another's body heat to keep them warm. With the darkness deepening, the cold continued to intensify. The noises in the town abated and, one by one, the oil lamps were lowered as people retired for the night.

Asinus had never felt more alone than he now felt in this icy stall, and he had seldom felt more resentful of human beings, all snugly asleep in their warm houses while their donkeys, outside in the cold, had to stay awake to keep from freezing. His new owners weren't freezing. He was sure of that. From their chimney he could still see smoke rising. Since Joseph was a carpenter, they probably had enough lumber scraps to keep a fire going all night, every night. If the man were half as concerned about his donkey as he pretended to be, would he not offer him a little of his heat?

While Asinus was thus ruminating bitterly, Joseph came out of the house, bundled in a sheepskin cloak, and hurried around to the stall. "Did you think I'd forgotten you?" he said. "Did you think I'd leave you

out in the open on a night like this? I had to clear a corner and make a bed for you. Come along. In by the fire before you freeze solid."

It was a boon Asinus felt guilty accepting. Was it possible he had actually misjudged Joseph and done him an injustice? He had to lower his head to walk through the door of the one-room house and, once inside, he took up so much of the space he made the room look even smaller than it was. Mary sat by the open hearth, sewing a garment in the dim light from the fire. A simple pine table with four chairs filled the center of the room. In one corner was a bed, covered with sheepskins. In the opposite corner was another bed, of straw, piled almost a foot high. Asinus went to it, rearranged it with his right hoof so it would fit the curves of his body, then settled down in it.

Mary said to Joseph, "I'm glad you brought him in. On a night as cold as this, you couldn't blame the poor thing if he were to run away."

Asinus, hearing this, found ample reason to cancel any gratitude he was beginning to feel. So that was why they had brought him in. Not to protect him from the cold, but simply to prevent him from escaping. He should have known they'd never do anything out of sheer generosity. After all, they were only human.

Why wasn't the wife doing the work? She was still in bed, but not asleep.

"Joseph, why didn't you wake me?" she said. "You've got to stop babying me. I'm having a child, that's all. I'm not sick."

He gazed at her adoringly, then went over to the bed and kissed her, but with more reverence than passion, as if she were a queen rather than his wife. "I don't want you carrying water and firewood," he said, helping her into a heavy robe as she got out of bed. Soon she was bustling about the tiny house, cooking gruel, straightening the few bits of furniture, sweeping the floor with a twig broom. As she swept her way toward the corner where Asinus lay in his bed of straw, still feigning sleep, she said, "It must be warmer this morning. It's not cold in here. I suppose you should put your new donkey outside, unless you really are afraid he'll run away."

"I'm not the least bit afraid he'll run away," Joseph said. "He's such a splendid specimen, I'm only afraid someone might steal him."

Mary put aside her broom, knelt down near the apparently sleeping donkey and ran her hand lightly along his flank, arousing in him an involuntary and even unwelcome tremor of warmth. "You were right, Joseph," she said. "Whatever you paid for him, he was worth it. But he will attract attention. He's so big! What if he were stolen? On the road, I mean. We might be stranded."

"Travelers don't steal from each other," Joseph assured her. "They help each other."

Asinus, hearing this, wondered where they thought they were going. Obviously south, but how far? To Jerusalem?

Joseph, after finishing his own breakfast, roused Asinus, led him out to his stall and fed him a delicious meal of hay and grain. When the donkey had eaten his fill, Joseph said, "Now to the shop. We've got work to do."

As soon as they entered the shop, Joseph began measuring Asinus's torso peculiarly, as if he were a tailor rather than a carpenter. He next produced a sheet of lumber almost two cubits square, created by joining several planks, and with a piece of charcoal, drew upon it an exact, or nearly exact, outline of the curve of the donkey's torso from his backbone halfway down each flank, so that the charcoal line looked like an arch drawn on the sheet of wood. With a small saw he cut out this arch, shaping the wood to fit as neatly as a saddle over Asinus's back. Then he produced another, identical sheet of wood, and after taking a second measurement of Asinus about a cubit behind the first, made a similar cutout.

"Do you know what I'm doing?" he asked the bemused donkey. "Well, I'll tell you. I won't have my wife riding sideways. Not in her condition. She's no ordinary woman. To me she's a queen, and she'll ride like a queen, in a proper chair. But don't worry, Asinus. This chair will fit you like your own hide. It'll be comfortable for both of you."

It took several moments for Asinus to digest all this. Though Mary was beautiful, she was hardly a queen.

She was a carpenter's wife. And a wife didn't ride a donkey. She led him and, in addition, carried everything she couldn't load onto him.

In the days that followed, Joseph completed the saddle chair, which for a fact did straddle Asinus's back quite comfortably, and did look, with its sheep-wool upholstery, as if it were made for a queen. When this job was done, the carpenter and his wife began visiting the shops and bazaars of Nazareth, with Asinus at their heels, to buy the provisions they would need. At one shop, Joseph saw a heavy cloak, of finest wool, which he proposed to buy for Mary. She said it was much too costly.

"The cloak I have will be quite enough," she insisted. "It served me well when I visited Elizabeth, and we'll be taking exactly the same route."

"But that was last summer," Joseph reminded her, "and you said yourself the nights were chilly even then."

"You mustn't squander your money," she said. But he bought it for her anyway, and when he draped it over her shoulders, her frown at his extravagance melted into a smile of comfort, and perhaps even of pride in this husband who cared so much for her welfare.

During their several days of shopping, they also bought some skins for water, two smaller flasks, bags of corn, flour, sugar and dried fruits, extra shoes for both of them, three bolts of heavy cloth, a gourd in which to draw water from the wells along the way and other useful items. In the evenings, sitting by the fire after prayers, Joseph would say to Mary, "Tell me again about your trip to see your cousin. Any mishaps along the way? Was the water sweet at all the wells? Was the road passable as far as Bethlehem? Could you always find an inn at nightfall?" He hadn't traveled very much himself, but she had apparently taken a trip just the previous summer all the way to the hills of Judah, near Hebron, twenty-five miles south of Jerusalem, where her cousin Elizabeth lived.

"The road is sometimes steep, sometimes narrow," Mary said, "and in the mountains it is so precipitous one might easily be afraid. They say there are floods and landslides, but we encountered none. They say also there are brigands hiding along the way, and wild beasts that attack at night, but we were never attacked. Our caravan was large, of course, and the men in it were brave. The water we drank was always sweet and plentiful. The inns were comfortable but usually crowded, perhaps because it was the best season to travel. Twice we had to sleep beneath the stars."

"You mean because there were no rooms at the inns? We mustn't let that happen to you on our journey."

By this time Asinus was aware that their destination was Bethlehem, a town just five miles south of Jerusalem. He knew it well because he had once spent some time there himself. Bethlehem, it seemed, was Joseph's ancestral home. And they actually were undertaking the journey to pay their taxes and register for the Roman census. Was this not enough in itself to prove Joseph hopelessly mad? Asinus, who didn't understand any man paying taxes to any government, was especially puzzled by Jews who paid taxes to the Romans. It was like paying for the privilege of being conquered. He had a low opinion of the Romans, not only because they were so pushy, and because they seemed to despise donkeys, largely preferring flashy horses, but also because his first owner had been a Roman. As a young jack not fully grown, he had been bought by an enterprising but foolish centurion, fresh from Rome, who had come up with a horse-brained scheme to make a lot of money in a short time. This centurion, arriving in Palestine with his legion, had noticed the absence of statuary and had decided he could get rich quick by importing statues from Rome to sell to the Jews. In due time, a consignment of plaster busts had arrived for the centurion at the port of·Joppa, and Asinus was one of several donkeys he had bought to carry the statues to Jerusalem, where he planned to offer them for sale. Asinus's connection with the enterprise lasted only through the first two attempts to load him down with statues, by which time the ground around him was littered with broken plaster. Even that early in life he had decided against a cargo-carrying career for himself. And he most assuredly was not willing to carry such a cargo. Besides being oppressively heavy, it was quite laughable. How would he explain to other donkeys along the way that he was carrying statues to a Jewish market?

One evening when Mary was clearing leftover bread from the table, she said to Joseph, "Don't you think it would be safer for us to travel in a caravan, as I did last summer? On the road we heard alarming stories of bandits attacking small groups of wayfarers."

Her husband put a comforting hand on hers. "You mustn't worry about everything you hear. Bandits attack wealthy men, not humble carpenters."

"You may not be wealthy," Mary replied, "but you'll be carrying all the money we'll need for travel, plus all the money you've saved for taxes. That is a very large sum."

"For people like us, indeed it is," he agreed.

"Then why do you object to traveling with a caravan?"

"I don't object," he said, "but I know of no caravan going south from Nazareth."

"There must be others here in Nazareth," Mary said, "who also come from southern families. Surely they'll have to make the same journey to pay their taxes."

"You may be right," Joseph said. "Perhaps I should ask around town."

The next evening Joseph announced happily that he had taken steps to allay Mary's fears. "Walking through the market today," he said, "I asked myself who among our fellow Nazarenes would be most likely to know about the comings and goings of travelers. And it struck me that of all men, a donkey dealer should be best informed about such things, since every traveler needs a donkey. So I paid another visit to the man from whom I bought Asinus. When I told him about the trip we're planning, he mentioned three men who are also planning such a trip. He promised to send them around. So you see, my dearest Mary, I've taken your advice. Perhaps we'll have company after all."

This news seemed to please Mary but it did not please Asinus. He could scarcely imagine any safety in traveling with three men who were friends of Ezekiel.

Joseph brought Asinus into his shop the next afternoon and was adjusting the cinches which held the saddle chair in place when there came a polite knock and a throat-clearing at the door. A short, slender man with wavy hair stood before them, clean-shaven and cleanly dressed in a dun-colored cloak. Behind him were two others, equally presentable; one of medium height but stocky and powerfully built, the other uncommonly tall and gangling. When they entered and stood beside each other, they looked like the steps of stairs.

"We are looking for a man named Joseph, a carpenter," the short one said, in round, unctuous tones.

"I am he," said Joseph.

"The same Joseph who's planning a trip to the south?"

"The very same. You gentlemen must be friends of Ezekiel, the donkey dealer."

"I wouldn't say we're friends. Ezekiel is not the kind of person a respectable man would choose as a friend. But he did tell us about you. He said you wanted to travel with a party of men, to ward off beasts and brigands and such."

Though Asinus was slightly relieved to hear them disavow friendship with Ezekiel, he still felt strong res-

ervations about the three men. The little one, who was doing the talking, had very quick eyes which seemed to dart in all directions, sizing up not only Joseph himself but everything in his shop. The other two, while they were fairly well dressed, as if they might be merchants, nevertheless looked uncomfortable in their clothes. They shifted from foot to foot. Their hands were constantly on the move. The stocky one kept clenching his fists. The tall one kept picking at his fingers. The stocky one was wide-faced and thick-lipped; the tall one was thin-faced and thin-lipped. Both had small eyes and brutish expressions. Though they might look like respectable merchants at first glance, Asinus, suspicious as usual, decided they were more likely to be thugs on their best behavior. And Asinus was not without experience at recognizing thugs, having been owned by several.

"For my part," Joseph said, "I would be quite at peace on the road with just my wife and my donkey, but my wife would be more comfortable, I think, if we traveled with others."

"And well she might," said the tall man. "With what things goes on these days, who can say the roads are safe?"

The short man glanced at his companion distastefully, then turned to Joseph with a smile. "I am Ichabod," he said. "My partners are Jabez, the tall, and Caleb, the stout, all three of us brick makers from Cana, heading south like yourself to pay our taxes. And our destinations, I understand, are almost the same. Your ancestral home is Bethlehem, is it not? Ours is Jerusalem."

"Splendid," Joseph said. "We shall much appreciate your company. Since you live in Cana, I'm surprised I haven't met you. I've been there many times. Where in Cana is your brickyard?"

Cana being only seven or eight miles from Nazareth, it was hardly surprising that Joseph knew the place well, yet the three seemed slightly taken aback by his question. Ichabod, their apparent spokesman, said, "Well, actually, we're not from Cana as such. We're just opening our brickyard there. Are you familiar with Capernaum?"

"Capernaum? No, that's beyond my territory. I'm a simple man. I've traveled little in my life."

"We could hardly expect you, then, to know us," Ichabod said. "Our main yard is in Capernaum. Upwards of a hundred men toil for us there."

"That means you're all quite wealthy," Joseph observed. "Why would you wish to travel with a poor carpenter?"

Caleb, the stout man, who had not yet spoken, said suddenly, "That ain't what Ezekiel told us."

He seemed about to continue when Ichabod cut him off. "Rich or poor, it doesn't matter on the road," he said. "All wayfarers are companions. We shall stand as brothers, ready to defend ourselves from any who might attack."

"Still, we are only four," Joseph said. "Let us hope we're not attacked."

Caleb broke in again. "And let them that might attack hope likewise. They get a taste of my scourge, they'll wish they hadn't. Look here." Producing a coiled whip from within his cloak, he pointed at the tools suspended from nails on the far wall of the shop. Lined up in a neat row were a hammer, a chisel, a rule, an awl and two saws. With six lightning-quick snaps of his scourge, Caleb knocked every one of them from its hook at a distance of almost five paces.

The moment Caleb finished this impressive demonstration, Jabez stepped forward. "Nobody gonna get close enough to feel Caleb's scourge," he announced. "Not while I'm around." Therewith he opened his cloak to reveal a wide leather belt in which a dozen or more daggerlike knives were sheathed. "So your name is Joseph," he said to the carpenter. "Well, Joseph, watch this."

Using both hands, he drew knives out of his belt, one after another, and threw them at a board against the far wall as quickly as Caleb had snapped his whip. When Jabez finished throwing, the daggers embedded in the wood formed a perfect letter G.

While he grinned proudly, the others looked puzzled. "You dumb oaf," Caleb said. "You don't spell Joseph with a G."

"Don't call me an oaf!" Jabez cried, drawing another knife from his belt.

"You're dumber than that donkey," Caleb bellowed, raising his scourge.

Ichabod, stepping between them, looked back at Joseph with a nervous smile on his face. "These two never get tired of teasing each other," he said. Asinus noticed, however, that he didn't smile at them. He stared coldly at one, then the other. They put away their weapons.

Joseph said, "For merchants, you gentlemen seem surprisingly skillful at defending yourselves."

"On the road nowadays," Ichabod said, "you have to be. Did not the prophet Ezekiel say, 'The land is full of bloody crimes and the city is full of violence'?"

"It pleases me to hear you quote the Scriptures," Joseph said, "but it was five or six hundred years ago that Ezekiel spoke those words."

"And did not God himself say that 'the wickedness of man was great in the earth'?"

"Yes, but that was right after the fall of Adam. Surely men are not so evil today as in the olden days."

"On the contrary," Ichabod argued, "the evils of corruption and vice, greed and intemperance, banditry and even murder are everywhere around us."

"In all my life," Joseph said, "I have not once been attacked by any man. I can't imagine someone trying to rob me. Yet such things happen, I guess."

"Which is exactly why honest men should travel together," Ichabod concluded.

"Is it agreed, then?" Joseph asked.

Ichabod said, "Nothing could please me more."

"But the way to Jerusalem is sometimes steep and narrow, they say, and often dangerous. Do you three know the route?"

"We know it," Caleb assured him, "like the way home from the wineshop."

"In a manner of speaking," Ichabod added hastily.

"We shall then be much indebted to you," Joseph said. "The only thing that remains is to choose the day of our departure. For my part, the earlier the better."

"I don't know about yourself, sir," Ichabod said, "but we are men of God. We wouldn't want to leave before the Sabbath."

"It pleases me beyond measure to hear that," Joseph said. "How about dawn, the day after the Sabbath?"

Without even nodding toward the other two, Ichabod said, "So be it."

As soon as the arrangements were completed, the three men left the shop and Joseph called Mary from the house to tell her the good news. He brought forth a bench for her but she declined to sit.

"I wish you'd stop fussing over me," she said. "I've become a figure of fun among the women around here. None of their husbands treat them so well."

"You can forget all your fears of beasts and brigands," he said. "We'll be traveling with three wealthy merchants from Capernaum. Partners in a brickyard there. And wonderfully skilled at defending themselves. In such company, my dear Mary, you will be as safe on the road as you would be at home."

Mary smiled and kissed him tenderly. "My darling Joseph, I don't care if they laugh at me. In all the world there is not a woman with a husband as marvelous as mine."

CHAPTER FIVE

T WAS A SIGHT THAT EARLY RISERS IN Nazareth would long remember— Mary, the carpenter's wife, a surpassingly beautiful woman, great with child, dressed in a robe of finest wool and seated comfortably on a sheep-wool covered chair atop a horse-sized gray-white donkey. Joseph walked ahead through the marketplace while three men—one short, one stout, one tall, neatly dressed and leading three other donkeys—followed in single file as if Mary were indeed a queen and they were her entourage. A silence fell over the busy street as they approached, and for several minutes little work was done as people watched this strange procession move on toward the southern end of town.

Though the small company of departing travelers looked almost majestic, one member of it, Asinus, was mortified by the many eyes upon him and his burden, which consisted not only of Mary in her chair but two bulky packs on each side behind her. Asinus could not overcome his shame at bowing so publicly to the will of a human being. But if he wanted his cherished freedom, he must accept this heavy load Joseph had put upon him, at least until nightfall when he would be able to slip away, unnoticed, into the far hills of Galilee.

The sun had taken the chill off the morning by the time they left Nazareth and began picking their way along the rocky trail down the long hill toward the Plain of Esdraelon. It was a trail deeply rutted, littered with boulders and in some places quite precipitous. To the surefooted Asinus, however, the road was the least of his worries. He didn't trust that trio behind them—Ichabod, Jabez and Caleb. He wished they were in front so he could watch them, but Ichabod had obsequiously declined Joseph's suggestion that he and his friends take the lead. "Your beautiful wife should lead us on her great white donkey," he said, "while we take up the rear, guarding her from danger." To Asinus, they looked like jackals guarding sheep.

When they reached the bottom of the Nazareth hill, they entered the most fertile plain in all of Palestine.

Large flocks of sheep and goats grazed on the slopes at its northern edge. Cypress, pine and carob trees dotted the landscape, which was still quite green despite the early winter. To right and left were vast olive and fig groves and vineyards, between fields that would lie fallow until spring planting. All of the first day's travel would be across this broad, pleasant valley, which meant it would be the easiest day of the entire journey.

Their destination for the night was an inn just off the road near Jezreel, a town on the side of Mount Gilboa about fifteen miles from Nazareth. It was a good one-day trek, but the route was smooth and fairly level. By midday, when they stopped for their bread and wine under a carob tree, they had already come more than halfway.

While the people were breaking bread, Asinus introduced himself to the other three donkeys, who were grazing with him on a grassy slope. Their names were Aaron, Amos and Hepzibah. They wondered about his name.

Aaron said, "It doesn't sound Jewish."

"It sounds Roman to me," said Amos. "You're not a Roman donkey, I hope."

"Oh no. It's just that my first owner was a Roman and I haven't been able to live it down."

"You're a handsome brute, anyway," said Hepzibah, a rather large brown jenny who had already passed her prime.

Amos said, "She thinks every jack donkey in the world is handsome."

"Present company excepted," Hepzibah said sharply.

"Tell me about your three friends, Ichabod, Jabez and Caleb," Asinus said. "They claim they're brick makers. Is that true?"

Aaron said, "Well, I guess you could say so."

"You mean they actually own a brickyard in Capernaum?"

At this, all three brayed. Amos said, "Capernaum? I don't think they've ever been that far north. They're from Jerusalem. But two of them, Jabez and Caleb, once did work in a brickyard, so I guess you could say they're brick makers."

"And did they learn to crack whips and throw knives in a brickyard?"

"No, they learned that," Hepzibah said, "on the highways."

"Just as I thought," Asinus said. "What are they planning for this carpenter?"

The three donkeys glanced at each other uncertainly. Hepzibah finally said to Aaron, "Tell him what you heard."

"Why should I?" he said. "If those devils don't come into some money pretty soon, we won't eat."

Asinus shook his head in exasperation. "Sometimes I think donkeys are as bad as people. Listen, I don't care about the larceny. I've lived my life around thieves. But those three look like real cutthroats. I'd like to know, at least, what they have in mind."

After some hemming and hawing, Aaron said, "I don't really know what they plan to do, but I think I know where they plan to do it. Have you ever traveled this road before?"

"Several times."

"Then you must know that deep gorge in the mountains between Jezreel and Engannim, where the road becomes just a narrow ledge on the side of the cliff. I heard Ichabod say that was the best place to do it. But he didn't say what they wanted to do."

Asinus felt immediately relieved at this news. "We couldn't possibly get that far before tomorrow afternoon."

"Just about."

"Well, then, I don't have to worry. I won't be with you tomorrow."

"What do you mean?"

"As soon as it gets dark tonight, I'm taking off into the hills. There's enough grass in those Galilee hills to feed half the donkeys in the world. There are places up there where human beings never go. It's a paradise."

"Ooh! Take me along!" Hepzibah exclaimed.

"I'd be glad to take all of you," Asinus said. "I don't want to get away from donkeys. I just want to get away from people."

Amos said, "Ah, that sounds tempting. But how could we manage it? They tie us to trees every night with heavy ropes."

"I'm not surprised," Asinus said. "Too bad you don't belong to my carpenter. He's so trusting he never ties me at all."

When the company set out after the midday meal,

the sun was so warm Mary was able to take off her cloak and drape it over the back of the saddle chair. "Why don't I walk awhile," she suggested, "and lighten Asinus's burden."

Joseph wouldn't hear of it. "I don't want you walking in your condition," he said, "and I'm sure Asinus doesn't either. Any donkey would be proud to carry a burden as lovely as you."

Finally she took her seat as Asinus fumed in silence at her husband. If Joseph was so proud of her, why didn't he carry her?

Since the road was fairly wide and smooth through the valley, Joseph walked along beside Asinus, talking to Mary. "How do you like our companions?" he asked her.

"I don't know," she said.

"I thought it was nice of them to offer us cakes after our meal. Tasty, weren't they?"

"Delicious," she said.

He waited but she said no more. "I get the feeling you have reservations about them."

"I haven't really talked to them," she said.

"Jabez and Caleb are rough-hewn, I'll admit, but Ichabod is well-spoken. He must come from a good family."

"Maybe so."

"Mary, there's something bothering you about them, isn't there?"

"Yes, I guess so."

"What is it?"

"I don't know."

He shook his head. "Sometimes, my dear, I think you're too suspicious."

Asinus felt a momentary touch of pity for Joseph. Though he was a human being, and therefore not worthy of a lot of sympathy, he didn't really deserve to be robbed by those thugs behind them. But what could Asinus do about that? In a way he would be helping Joseph and Mary by escaping from them tonight. Without him, they wouldn't get to that gorge in the mountains where Ichabod, Jabez and Caleb apparently intended to rob them.

Despite the afternoon warmth, the road was sparsely traveled. Winter was not a popular season for journeys. Only three or four times an hour did they pass people going the other way, and they had not yet overtaken, or been overtaken by, anyone going their way. Joseph was glad of this. "With the road so empty," he said to Mary, "we should have no trouble finding room at that inn."

The sun had just disappeared behind Mount Carmel when they came to the crossroad leading up to Jezreel. The inn they sought was one Mary had remembered from her journey the previous summer. Nestled among oak and sycamore trees on a slope about a quarter of a mile up the Jezreel road, it was more comfortable than most caravansaries. Several of its rooms were private, and in addition to beds, they were furnished each with a table, chair and candle. There was also a loggia for travelers who could not afford rooms, but when Mary suggested they stay there to save money, Joseph wouldn't hear of it. Ichabod, Jabez and Caleb also took a room, which they shared. It was so small Joseph wondered how three men could fit into it. "For wealthy merchants," he said to Mary, "they seem wonderfully frugal. I admire them for that."

Ichabod, Jabez and Caleb tied their donkeys securely in the yard, but on long tethers so they could reach a patch of rich grass. "You see, they don't treat us so badly," Amos said to Asinus, who was grazing untethered beside them.

"What was that thumping sound I heard behind me this afternoon?" Asinus asked. "It sounded to me like a stick meeting a donkey's backside."

"Yes, but a lot of men do that. These fellows at least find good grass for us at the end of a day."

"Otherwise they might have to buy feed for you. What are you trying to tell me? That you've decided not to run away with me?"

"I'd love to escape," Aaron said, "but are you sure we'd like it up there in the hills, all by ourselves? It must get pretty cold at night. And I hear the grass isn't really that green."

"I'd go in a minute," Hepzibah said, "but how can I with this tether holding me back?"

"You could chew through the rope."

"Do you think so? Look how thick it is."

"It sounds to me," Asinus said, "as if you're all afraid to make a break for it."

"Nobody's holding you back," Amos pointed out. "Why don't you go?"

"Not until dark," Asinus said. "If you run away

while it's still daylight, and everyone's up and about, the whole countryside will be after you. I made that mistake the last time I tried to escape, in Nazareth."

It was almost dark now. Ichabod, Jabez and Caleb emerged from the inn apparently to make sure their donkeys were secure for the night. Seeing Asinus, they stopped to take a close look at him.

Caleb said, "Ain't he the biggest donkey you ever saw?"

"I can see why the carpenter bought him," Jabez said. "I'd buy him if I didn't know about him."

"But would you pay twelve shekels? For a runaway! That carpenter's gotta be as dumb as he is rich."

"He'd better be as rich as he is dumb," Ichabod said, "or we're wasting a lot of time."

"Hey, look!" Caleb exclaimed. "He forgot to tie the beast up for the night."

Jabez said, "Maybe he trusts him."

"A runaway donkey? You're as dumb as he is."

While Jabez and Caleb argued, Ichabod slipped in close to Asinus and got a firm hold on his headstall. Turning to Caleb, he said, "Shut up and go get that chain you brought with you."

Asinus, realizing he was in trouble, bucked and reared and yanked in a desperate effort to get away, but Jabez came running to the aid of Ichabod and grabbed the other side of his headstall. In the fierce struggle that ensued, Asinus was able to stomp on each of their feet a few times, and even landed one good sideways kick on Jabez's upper leg. He could not, however, fight his way free of the two men. Caleb

soon appeared with a length of chain and Asinus was tethered even more securely than the other donkeys.

Exhausted from their struggle, Ichabod and Jabez sat down against a tree to nurse their bruises. "I'd like to kill that beast," Jabez swore. "Hey, Caleb, take a stick and give him a few good licks for me, will you?"

Caleb, who had not been much involved in the struggle except when he fastened the chain to Asinus's headstall, nevertheless willingly picked up a heavy cudgel and, with evil in his eyes, approached the helpless donkey.

"Leave him alone," Ichabod commanded.

Caleb stopped and gaped at him. "Why?"

"Because we need him tomorrow. If he's crippled in the morning, how can he carry those two up into the mountains?"

Caleb said, "I never thought of that."

"You never think of anything. If we fail on this job, you can forget all your dreams about the fun we'll have in Jerusalem."

"Yeah, but what if Ezekiel was wrong?" Jabez suggested. "What if this carpenter's got no money?"

"Zeke saw his purse," Ichabod reminded him. "And Zeke knows silver when he sees it. Besides, the whole purpose of his journey is to pay his taxes, so he has to have money."

"When we get through with him," Caleb said, "he won't have no taxes to pay."

"Only if we do it right," Ichabod warned.

Jabez said, "I can't wait to get rid of them. Then I

can have my revenge on this vicious donkey. I'm gonna change him from white to black-and-blue."

Ichabod said, "No you won't."

"Why not?"

"Because I don't want anyone to come along and find the donkey still with us. How can we explain why they fell off the cliff if the donkey didn't fall?"

Jabez said, "You mean we gotta push the donkey off, too?"

"Of course. Then when all three bodies are found together, people will blame the donkey. They'll think he lost his footing."

A prolonged shudder racked Asinus's body as he overheard this hideous conversation. He almost wished he had taken his chances with Ezekiel. These devils were even worse, and there were three of them. Though he had suspected they were cutthroats, he could not have believed they could perpetrate such foul murders simply to steal a purse. The evil in men's hearts never ceased to amaze this proud donkey.

CHAPTER SIX

WHEN THE COMPANY ASSEMBLED SHORTLY after dawn the next morning for the second day of the journey, Joseph was surprised first to find Ichabod and Jabez limping noticeably, and then to find Asinus in chains. Ichabod was quick to explain. "I'm afraid you forgot to tether your donkey," he said, "and when we set about doing it for you, the beast kicked like the devil and stomped on our feet. But we got the chain on him just the same. We didn't want him running away from you during the night."

"That was considerate," Joseph said, "but you

needn't have tethered him. I never do. He won't run away as long as I treat him decently."

Caleb said, "I don't know about that. I've had donkeys to run away from me, and God knows I treat 'em good."

"Yeah, donkeys just love to run away," Jabez added. "They like people. And they ought to. Look how we feed 'em. But they're dumb, that's all."

"Then how come you don't run away?" said Caleb.

"These two never stop kidding each other," Ichabod said to Joseph.

Though Asinus was vaguely aware of Aaron, Amos and Hepzibah trying to catch his eye during this conversation, he was too depressed, nervous and frightened even to exchange knowing glances with them. His brain was racing around in search of a way to save his life. He was doomed if he let them lead him up into those mountains ahead, but how could he avoid it? Maybe he should refuse to move. What then? Ichabod, Jabez and Caleb, with Joseph's approval, would beat him. Joseph could talk about treating a donkey decently, but if the donkey refused to carry his load, he'd be just like any other man. And especially since the load happened to be his beloved wife. Depending on Joseph's decency in these circumstances would be as useless as praying for a snowstorm to close the mountain roads on a bright, sunny day like this one.

Joseph appeared to be in the best of spirits. He had a cheery word for each of his traveling companions, including the four donkeys, to whom he also gave handfuls of grain he had apparently bought from the innkeeper. "I see we're all blowing a bit of steam this morning," he said. "But it's not really cold, thank God. Just cool enough to make a person want to get up and move. What a beautiful day. Look at the sun coming up above Mount Gilboa. And look to the west. Mount Carmel, the Sacred Promontory, where Elijah defeated the heathen prophets. See how it sparkles with the sun upon it, as if God had taught it to smile. I understand now why people love to travel. When shall we have a day more pleasant than yesterday, unless it might be today."

"If all goes well," Ichabod said, glancing at Caleb and Jabez, "today will be much better than yesterday."

"Only if murder is one of your pleasures," Asinus said in an aside to Hepzibah.

"I can't think of anything Ichabod enjoys more," she said. And Asinus could see she was serious.

"You mean you've seen him kill others?"

"Several."

"But he wouldn't have to kill just to rob somebody. It's easy to steal a purse. I used to be owned by a pickpocket who could lift a man's money while bidding him good day."

"But Ichabod is different. For him there's more fun in the killing than in the robbing."

The first hour or so of this morning's travel was an easy walk as the little party skirted Mount Gilboa and crossed the south side of the valley. But with the central highlands looming ahead, the road steepened and began to wind through barren soil with outcroppings of large rocks. As they entered the mountains through a narrow gap, Joseph stopped to gaze in wonder at the green beauty of the canyon floor, the rapid creek rushing toward the valley behind them and the high canyon walls rising sharply on both sides. "I feel as if I'm entering a temple," he said to Mary, "but a greater temple than man could ever build. Surely even the Temple of Jerusalem cannot be as beautiful as this one. God himself built these towering columns of stone."

"Yet the Temple of Jerusalem is a marvel to behold," Mary said.

"Ah yes, you've seen it. And will again, and so shall I in just a few days. At this rate, we should reach Jerusalem easily before the Sabbath. Can you imagine, my darling, the awe that fills your humble husband, first at being chosen to watch over a woman so special as yourself, and then at being allowed to see such marvels as these mountains, and the great Temple, and the city of Jerusalem and all the other wondrous sights ahead of us? Never did I dream that I would one day be chosen for such honors and such joys."

As Joseph talked, Asinus felt his patience dwindling. Will the man never shut up so I can think, he wondered. We've got four or five hours to live, and he's talking about the marvels he plans to see next week.

Blotting Joseph from his mind, he resumed concentrating on the three men behind him until, gradually, the significance of the very word "behind" sank into his brain and gave birth to an idea. Though they were no more than fifteen cubits behind, that might be enough. Asinus had at least the advantage of knowing the exact spot where they intended to commit their foul deed. And he was undoubtedly faster afoot than any of them or any of their donkeys. If he were to break into a run as they approached the place where the road was narrowest and the gorge deepest, wouldn't Joseph have to chase him at full speed? It wasn't a foolproof plan. It would be thwarted if the three scoundrels, after a stop for the midday meal, were to take the lead for a change. But it was at least a promising plan, and such a simple one he felt foolish for taking so long to think of it.

He resumed listening to Joseph and Mary when he heard one of them mention his name. It was Mary, talking about how comfortable she was in her chair atop him, what a surefooted beast he was, how smoothly and gently he carried her.

"He was not so gentle, I guess, with our friends last night," Joseph said, "but I suppose you couldn't blame him for resisting the chain. Nobody should be chained. All God's creatures should be free. Just the same, it was very nice of the three of them to be concerned about us. I'm beginning to like them, aren't you?"

"I'd like to know more about them," Mary said.

"I was sorry to learn Asinus had stomped on their feet. Poor Ichabod and Jabez, they could hardly walk this morning."

This reminder of what he had done to Ichabod and Jabez exhilarated Asinus. There's another thing, he said to himself, that ought to help my plan. They'll have a hard time running after me on their swollen feet. I should have gotten in a few licks at Caleb.

During the midday break, Asinus hardly tasted the grain Joseph put before him. He could concentrate on nothing but his escape plan. The morning's climb had been up a fairly wide road and they had stopped to eat at a V-shaped recess in the mountains where the ground was almost level. But Asinus remembered from previous journeys that as the canyon became ever higher and the route ever steeper ahead of them, the road would gradually close in against the mountain wall until it became only a perilously narrow shelf on the face of the towering cliff. Joseph had never traveled this dangerous road, and he wasn't destined to travel more than half of it if Ichabod, Jabez and Caleb managed to carry out their plot. Asinus's fragile plan seemed the only hope of thwarting them now, but it wouldn't work if they decided they should begin leading the way. It would be impossible to get past them when the crucial moment arrived, and equally impossible, on that slender ledge, to turn around so he could flee the other way.

After the four donkeys and five people had finished eating and the time had come to resume their journey, Asinus became increasingly nervous. Would Ichabod, Jabez and Caleb take the lead? Or would his luck hold? He wished he had fingers to cross. The three scoundrels, all of whom seemed to eat more quickly than Mary and Joseph, came first to get their donkeys. Passing Asinus, they stopped to glower at him.

Caleb looked around to make sure Joseph couldn't hear him. "Zeke was right," he said. "That's the meanest donkey in all Palestine."

"I can hardly wait to push him off the cliff," Ichabod added. "My feet are still killing me."

Asinus looked down at Caleb's feet, the only ones he hadn't yet damaged. They were about a cubit from his own front hooves. It would take just a quick step sideways to stomp on his left toes. With two quick moves, it might even be possible to put hoofprints on both feet before Caleb managed to back away. Planting himself carefully, Asinus raised his right front hoof and was about to stomp down when Joseph arrived to spoil his chance.

"Well, gentlemen," he said, "I see you're getting along better with my donkey today."

Ichabod said, "We were just admiring him."

"I'm sorry he stepped on your toes last night, but I'm sure he's also sorry. He would never want to hurt anyone. Would you, Asinus?"

Turning toward Hepzibah, the frustrated Asinus said, "There are moments when I'd be glad to see this fellow go off the cliff if I didn't have to follow him." But when they formed up and moved out, he forgot his annoyance at Joseph because Ichabod, Jabez and Caleb fell in behind them as usual. His plan was still intact.

As they climbed higher along the ever-narrowing

ledge, the vegetation became sparser—mostly scrubby terebinth that looked as if goats had been eating at it —until eventually there was almost no greenery at all. On the face of the mountain above them to the right, there was only bare rock, some of which was apparently quite loose, since the roadway was littered with fallen boulders. Here and there, against the steep slope on the inside of the path, were piles of loose rock that had come down from above. Noticing one such pile, Asinus began to have hopeful visions of rockslides ahead. But looking ahead he could see that, despite the boulders strewn in their path, and the occasional rock piles along the inner edge of it, there was no indication that their passage might be blocked.

There were coming ever closer now to the place where the gorge was deepest and the cliff most precipitous below them. Asinus wished he had eyes in the back of his head so he could watch the treacherous trio behind him and make sure they didn't sneak up on him. Not knowing exactly when they would make their move, he decided it was time to make his. Only about three hundred cubits ahead was the apex of the cliff, the ideal place for Ichabod to strike.

Drifting to the outside of the path, Asinus prepared to break into a run. But alas, before he could slip past Joseph, the man grabbed his headstall.

"Oh no, Asinus!" he exclaimed, pulling him firmly back to the inside. "It's too dangerous near the edge."

Asinus's heart sank. What could he do now? He'd have to wait for Joseph to let go of his headstall, then make his dash. But Joseph didn't let go. "I think I'd better keep hold of him for a while," he said to Mary. "This road is narrower than I imagined. Poor thing, I thought he had better sense than to go that near the brink."

To Asinus this was the crowning insult. He tries to save a man from murder and the man tells him he doesn't have good sense. He snapped his head from side to side in an effort to break away from Joseph, but to no avail. Joseph was strong, and he was determined not to let go of a suddenly rebellious donkey who was carrying his wife.

"Take it easy," he said soothingly, without even raising his voice. "Calm down, Asinus. There's nothing wrong." Glancing up at Mary he said, "Something must have frightened him. Maybe he saw a snake. But don't worry, my dear, he'll be all right."

By this time Asinus had already stopped struggling, having concluded that he couldn't break free. What then could he do? At any moment, Ichabod, Jabez and Caleb would come running up to murder all three of them. There was nothing left now but to wait until that happened and hope to make a run for it while they struggled with Joseph—assuming Joseph would at least struggle. Asinus could imagine him going off the cliff, still convinced they meant him no harm.

Asinus was reflecting dismally in this vein when he noticed on the inside of the road ahead a high and very steep delta of rocks that were leaning precariously against the face of the mountain. At the bottom of this pile was one large, round boulder, about a cubit in diameter, that looked as if it were the cornerstone supporting everything above it. He wondered. Was the pile as unstable as it appeared to be? It was stacked so high, rock upon rock, against the mountain, that if it were to come down, it would completely block the path.

Though he was unable to turn his head with Joseph holding his headstall, he could now hear the footsteps of Ichabod, Jabez, Caleb and their donkeys closing in behind him. Aside from their footsteps, which came ever closer without sounding hurried, the three men were silent. Only Hepzibah's braying voice broke the unbearable stillness: "You'd better do something quick, Asinus!"

The last desperate moment had arrived. Clinging to the inside of the road under Joseph's restraint, he walked so close to the round cornerstone boulder he almost touched it. Just as he passed, he sneezed with all his might, thus distracting Joseph from the fact that at the same time he had come to a sudden stop, directly in front of the boulder. Summoning all the force he could muster, he gave that rock an explosive shove with both hind legs, then stepped forward and resumed his normal gait as if nothing had happened.

"Bless you!" cried Joseph, reacting to the sneeze but blissfully unaware of the more important event behind him until he heard the rocks begin to fall. In his astonishment at this thunderous noise, he let go of Asinus and turned to investigate. The round, Asinus-powered boulder, rolling downhill, had knocked Caleb for a loop, pitching him over the edge of the precipice so

that he was hanging in space but still clinging to the ledge by his fingertips. Ichabod, Jabez and the three donkeys had escaped the rolling stone by leaping to the inside of the ledge. They were now totally separated from Joseph, Mary and Asinus by an avalanche of rocks that the loosened cornerstone had brought down to block the road.

Everyone seemed paralyzed by the sudden disaster until Caleb's terrified shrieks began. "Help!" he screamed. "Help! Help! Help!"

Joseph said to Mary, "I can't stand by and let him fall."

Scrambling up the perilously steep pile of loose rocks, he made a valiant effort to get over the top of it so he could rush to the rescue. Before he even approached the top, the rocks on which he was stepping fell away, depositing him, not over the cliff edge as one might expect, but, through the grace of whatever good fortune seemed always to follow him, right back with Mary and Asinus, where he had started.

By this time, Ichabod and Jabez, on their side of the rockslide, had picked their way between scattered boulders to the cliff's edge and, each grabbing one arm, pulled their comrade to the relative safety of the ledge.

"Is he all right?" Joseph shouted as he watched them raise Caleb to his feet. Though rumpled, dusty and trembling with fright, he showed no signs of being severely damaged. Ichabod was soon ignoring him and shouting back across the rockslide to Joseph.

"You want my advice, you'll get rid of that donkey!"

Joseph was puzzled. "Get rid of Asinus? Whatever for?"

"He's a troublemaker. He caused the slide. Kicked that rock out from under."

"I'm sure you're mistaken," Joseph said. "I was right beside him. He was sneezing when it happened."

"Sneezing!" Ichabod exclaimed. "Has it come to pass that a donkey can sneeze through his hooves?"

"The question is," Joseph said, "can we clear the road and get ourselves reunited before nightfall? We'd better start pushing rocks over the cliff. You start from your side and I'll start from mine."

Asinus was thoroughly bemused as he watched Joseph begin pitching boulders. Did the man actually intend to spend the rest of the day, and perhaps most of tomorrow, working the skin off his hands, just to give those three villains another chance to kill him? Fortunately, there was an easy way to persuade him to change his mind about that.

After one last glance at Joseph, and at the three men on the other side of the avalanche, all busily heaving boulders off the cliff, Asinus turned slowly to avoid alarming Mary, then broke into a trot uphill toward the summit of the narrow road, about two hundred cubits ahead.

Mary, grabbing his headstall, cried, "Whoa, Asinus! Whoa!"

Since he paid no attention, she continued to pull back on the headstall and at the same time leaned forward, caressing his neck. "Stop, Asinus. Don't be frightened. The danger is past."

That's what you think, he said to himself, increasing his speed as he approached the summit.

Behind him he heard Caleb bellowing at Joseph, "Hey! There goes your donkey!"

"And your wife!" Jabez added.

"Asinus!" Joseph cried in alarm. "Come back, Asinus!"

"I warned you about him!" Ichabod shouted.

Asinus now broke into a gallop. As he reached the summit and started down the road in the direction of Engannim, he could still hear behind him the plaintive voice of Joseph in pursuit: "Wait, Asinus! Wait!"

By the time Joseph reached the summit, Asinus was so far ahead he could safely slow his pace. He didn't want to get out of sight. If he were to lose Joseph completely, how would he ever get rid of this woman on his back? He wanted simply to stay far enough ahead so Joseph couldn't catch him, at least until they reached Engannim where, as he knew, Joseph and Mary planned to spend the night. As soon as they found an inn and relieved him of the burden he was carrying, he would settle down in a nearby field, graze until nightfall, then finally make the escape he had been planning since the day Joseph bought him. He had to get away from this innocent carpenter. It was more difficult to cope with his simple virtues than it had been to cope with the complex vices of other men who had owned him.

When Joseph finally caught up, a few minutes before sunset, on the outskirts of the village of Engannim, he was too concerned about his wife and too exhausted from his long chase to castigate his runaway donkey, who now stood quietly by the side of the road, munching on a clump of grass.

"Mary! Are you all right?" the distraught man cried between gulps of air.

Still sitting on her chair atop Asinus, she put out a hand to her husband. "Oh, Joseph, Joseph, why do you put up with me? I don't even know how to stop a donkey. I've made you run your heart out."

"Don't worry about me. What about you?"

"Believe me, I tried to stop him. He was just determined to run."

"It must have been a terrible ordeal."

"An ordeal? For me?" She seemed amazed at the suggestion. "Not at all."

"How did you hold on? I was afraid he'd throw you."

"Asinus? Never. It was the fastest ride of my life, I must admit, but also the smoothest."

"You're sure you're not hurt?"

"Not a scratch."

Eventually reassured, Joseph turned for the first time to Asinus. He ran his hand along the donkey's shoulder. "I wonder what got into him. He must have been terribly frightened by something."

Mary said, "It was the rockslide, don't you think?"

"It must have been, yet he didn't bolt when it happened. It was at least five minutes later. I'm afraid I'll never understand how donkeys think."

He's right about that, Asinus said to himself.

After making inquiries as they passed through Engannim, they found an inn on the road just a mile south of the town. It was larger than the place at which they'd stayed the previous night. It had a stable attached and the adjacent fields were lush with grass. As soon as Asinus was relieved of his burden and turned loose, he began munching his way across one of those fields. He was tired from his long run and chilly now that the sun was down. Tonight would be colder than last night, but he didn't care. He was happy in the knowledge that he would soon be free. He looked up for only a moment to watch Joseph and Mary disappear into the inn. It was the last time he would ever see them. For human beings, they weren't bad. But with all their apparent decency, they were still people, and people were his enemies. He must never forget it.

He was surveying the hills a half hour later, trying to choose the best escape route, when he found that he hadn't quite seen his owners for the last time. They came out to get Mary's saddle chair, which they had left on the loggia while they were settling into their room. Joseph picked up the chair and Mary was holding the door open for him when he said something to her, put down the chair and came out into the field.

"Asinus!" he called. "Come here, Asinus!"

What now, the donkey wondered. Should he respond or should he turn and run? It wasn't quite dark. If he ran now, he'd be chased immediately and he'd get no head start on his pursuers. No. After waiting this long, he mustn't spoil his plan by making a premature move. Walking over to the carpenter, he rubbed his nose against the man's shoulder.

Joseph gave him an affectionate hug. "You know, you frightened me today, Asinus. But you were careful with Mary, and I love you for that. Come along. I want to give you a treat."

Taking hold of the donkey's headstall, he led him toward the inn. Before Asinus knew where he was going, he found himself entering the stable connected to it.

"Will you give this donkey some nice fresh grain," Joseph said to the groom, "and a stall for the night? It's altogether too cold for him outside."

As the stable door closed behind him, Asinus realized, to his chagrin, that his escape plans had been foiled once more.

CHAPTER SEVEN

VER MINDFUL THAT ICHABOD, JABEZ AND
Caleb were not far behind, that having
cleared the road they might already be pressing down
upon them in murderous pursuit, Asinus was eager to
get away early the third morning of the journey. Joseph, on the other hand, ever mindful that he had lost
the company of these traveling companions just as he
was getting to know them, felt quite disposed to wait
for them.

"I'm afraid I let our friends down yesterday," he said
to Mary when they came out to the stable to get Asi-

nus. "The minute they needed my help, I had to run off after you. I'd like to make it up to them. I owe them at least an apology. Maybe we should wait for them. Better yet, you could stay here at the inn for a day of rest while Asinus and I go back and see if they still need help. Do you good to take a day off. We'll still get to Jerusalem before the Sabbath."

Fortunately, Mary pointed out that in her condition she should not spend any more days on the road than necessary. Asinus was much relieved when Joseph bowed without argument to this sensible observation. But even when they got on the road, Joseph's guilt at having abandoned their friends was evident. Asinus, pressing to stay ahead of them, set the fastest pace he thought Joseph would tolerate. It turned out to be a faster pace than Joseph could handle. "I don't know what's got into our donkey lately," he said to Mary. "Yesterday he was determined to gallop. Today he seems determined at least to trot. Slow up, Asinus. Our friends will never catch us if we go this fast."

To prevent Joseph from putting a lead on him and restraining him forcibly, Asinus would diminish his pace for a while, until Joseph's mind was on something else, then gradually increase it again until Joseph, notified of their speed by his own shortness of breath, would slow him up once more. Under this jerky but still rapid regimen, they had covered more than ten miles and had crossed the Plain of Dothan, plus a ridge of hills south of it, by midday. Though Joseph's aim was to get only as far as the environs of Mount Ebal that night, a few miles north of the Samarian city of Shechem, Asinus was determined to get as far as Shechem, a sizable town in which a man, a woman and a donkey might be difficult to find.

Throughout the afternoon, Joseph would turn and look back each time they came to a high point in the road, hoping to see the three men approach from the rear. "I wish they'd catch us," he said to Mary. "I miss them. Don't you?"

Mary said, "I'm quite content with you and Asinus."

He studied her. "You don't like those men, do you?"

"I didn't say that. It's just that I'm not entirely comfortable with them."

"But you must have some sympathy for them. They probably slept the night on that cold, narrow ledge while we slept warm and snug at Engannim. Surely you feel sorry about that."

"Indeed I do," she said. "But I feel safer without them."

"Safer? Why?"

"Because I trust you and Asinus more than I ever trusted them."

Joseph shook his head. "It was you," he reminded her, "who said we'd be safer if we had company on the road."

"Yes, but that depends on the company."

"Well, what's wrong with Ichabod, Jabez and Caleb?"

"I wonder if they really own a brickyard in Capernaum?"

"They said so. Why should they lie?"

"And I wonder if they're as God-fearing as you

thought they were. Have you ever heard them pray?"

"Prayer is a private matter," Joseph said. "Why should they pray in front of me? I don't pray in front of them."

"I do," she said. "I whisper 'God help us' every time one of them comes close."

They crossed another fairly level plain from which they could look up the rocky hill on their right at the old royal city of Samaria, built by King Omri almost nine hundred years earlier. Olive trees, perhaps several hundred years old themselves, rose up around the town's ancient ruins. Other than these trees, there was little greenery to relieve the bleakness of the parched, barren land through which they were passing. Occasionally they would encounter small groups of other travelers, trudging northward. "God's blessings upon you," Joseph would cry out to them. "May He hold back rain and flood, snow and cold until you're safely home."

Skirting the northern reaches of Mount Ebal in mid-afternoon, they now climbed toward the highlands of Ephraim and approached Shechem which, thanks to Asinus's rapid pace, had become their destination for the night. On the right, to the south, was Mount Gerizim. Shechem, nestled in the narrow pass between Ebal and Gerizim, was no longer the proud stronghold it had been in ancient times, but it was still a bustling town, an important stopping place on the hill road connecting Galilee with the south. It was also, in keeping with an ancient tradition, a sanctuary town where fugitives from other towns could come for ref-

uge, presumably until they were able to prove themselves innocent of the crimes for which they had been
charged. Since many of these fugitives were slow to
establish their innocence, sometimes because of the
number of people who had witnessed their guilt,
Shechem had become a haven for unsavory charac-
ters who preyed upon trustful travelers. Asinus knew
the place fairly well because he had once been sold
there. He was owned at the time by a Jericho jute
merchant who brought him along on a trip north because he couldn't sell him in Jericho, where Asinus's
obstinacy had become legendary. Strangely enough,
this was how Asinus had come to live for a time in
Bethlehem. The jute dealer, while in Shechem, had
managed to pass him off on a tyrannical and crooked
Bethlehem rug dealer, who happened to be going
through town on his way home, having rid himself of
about thirty donkey-loads of spurious Persian carpets
during a tour of Galilee. Before the rug dealer bought
him, Asinus had made one of his periodic escape attempts and, by the time he was caught, had become
well acquainted with the streets of Shechem as well as
the riffraff who frequented them. Remembering some
of the rogues and rascals he had seen there, he
couldn't help wondering what adventures might be in
store for a man like Joseph.

As they trudged up the winding path toward the city
gate, Joseph gazed at it in wonder. "Since I was a boy
I've been hearing about the old walls of Shechem," he
said, "but I didn't think I'd ever see them."

The stone walls of Shechem, topped by a continuous row of battlements, were indeed impressive, stretching left and right almost to the limits of the mountain pass they occupied. Through the single gate in the center a flow of people passed in both directions. A guard looked down from directly above this gate, which was flanked by high towers more than twenty cubits wide. Whole companies of soldiers could take defensive positions there in the olden days when Shechem was a strategically important fortress, but no soldiers were in evidence now.

Inside the town, the market streets were filled with swarms of people and the din of shouting voices filled the air as merchants hawked their wares. So many peddlers and hustlers rushed forward that a newly arriving traveler could walk scarcely ten or fifteen cubits without being accosted by someone who either wanted or offered something. By the time Joseph had reached the center of the town, he had politely declined to buy jewels, rings, necklaces, silks, linens, harps, drums, sandals, cloaks, buckets, bread, cakes, tools, jars, lamps, tents, olives, figs, mirrors, daggers, slings and scourges. He resisted peddlers and shopkeepers so steadfastly that Asinus began to think he wasn't such an easy mark after all. But as they entered the crowded town square, he was stopped by three ragged beggars before whom his resistance faded immediately. The first was wearing an eye patch and seemed to have only one arm beneath his tattered robe. The second had most of his head swathed in a filthy brown bandage with openings only for one eye and his mouth. The third was supporting his twisted body on an equally twisted walking stick. Without hesitation, Joseph reached inside his cloak, brought forth his purse, loosened the strings and produced a coin for each of them.

"May God bless you and heal you," he said, shaking his head sadly at their infirmities.

As he walked on, returning his purse to its hiding place, a neat, clean-looking young man in a heavy gray cloak, who had witnessed his act of charity, fell in step with him. "I noticed your generosity," he said. "You must be a kind and decent man."

"I hope so," Joseph said, "and I thank you."

"But I feel I should warn you. This town is full of people who will take advantage of you."

"Thank you again. I'll be on my guard."

"Beggars especially," the man continued. "Those three to whom you opened your purse—do you really think they're as unfortunate as they look?"

"Those poor creatures back there? They were pathetic," Joseph declared. "One was hideously crippled, one was grievously injured, and the third was almost blind. He seemed to have lost an arm as well."

"So it looked, but I can tell you, kind sir, I know those three. When night falls, they drop their crutches, take off their bandages, cast aside their rags and go home to big brick houses where their wives are at this very moment cooking fresh bread for them and laying out fine wines. Beneath those tattered robes, they're dressed in silks and linens, all three of them."

Joseph stopped and stared at him agape. "Are you certain of that?"

"All too certain, I fear. But maybe I shouldn't have said it. I didn't want to upset you. I wanted only to put you on the alert so no one else will deceive you."

At that moment, a man on a donkey came galloping toward them and passed so close to Joseph he might well have hit him had not the stranger grabbed him and pulled him aside.

Asinus, who had been puzzled by the man's overly solicitous behavior, suddenly saw through it. Having been owned once by a pickpocket, he was quite familiar with the galloping-donkey ruse. He could see that the man was putting Joseph's leather purse in the right-hand pocket of his cloak even as he helped him regain his equilibrium. Shaking his fist at the speeding donkey rider, the man said to Joseph, "I'll catch that reckless devil for you!" And with that he was off down the street, supposedly in pursuit of the donkey.

"Wait! Don't go!" Joseph shouted after him. "I haven't thanked you for saving my life!"

Asinus, witnessing all of this, wondered what he should do now. I can't run after that scamp with this woman on my back. And her husband won't run after him. He doesn't even suspect he's been robbed. How can I tell him?

Joseph pressed onward to the center of the square, where he stopped to look around at the women gossiping near the well, and at the children playing nearby and at the old men sitting idly on stone benches. He gazed at the shops, teeming with people, at the ruins of an ancient temple and at the flat-roofed houses which looked like steps of stairs against the hills on both sides.

"Do you know," he said to Mary, "that Abraham visited this town two thousand years ago?"

Mary smiled. "I believe I've heard it mentioned."

"And that this is where Joshua read the law to the assembled multitude?"

"Yes, dear. 'Half of them over against Mount Gerizim and half of them over against Mount Ebal.' You see? We women also read the Scriptures."

Joseph didn't seem to hear her. "It's a place I've often wished I could come to pray," he said.

Asinus thought to himself, You've got reason to pray. Wait till you reach for your purse.

The image of Joseph doing just that gave Asinus an idea as to how he could inform the man he had been robbed. Not far away he saw another beggar sitting on the ground with palms outstretched. While Joseph continued to daydream, Asinus turned and, with Mary still on his back, walked over to the beggar.

Mary said, "Asinus! What are you doing?"

A moment later, Joseph came running after them.

Mary, looking down at the beggar, then at Joseph, cried, "Oh no! You must stop giving money away, Joseph. You're not a wealthy man. Look what you've got our donkey doing. The minute he sees a beggar, he walks right up to him. He just assumes you'll want to give him something."

"Well, why not?" Joseph said, reaching inside his cloak for his purse. "God will always provide for . . ."

His hand reached deeper inside his cloak. His mouth dropped open. He put both hands inside his cloak where they could be seen scurrying back and forth across his belly.

Mary said, "What's the matter, dear?"

He looked up at her in consternation. "I can't believe it!" he cried. "I seem, I seem, I seem to have dropped my purse." Without another word, he rushed back to the fountain, then continued retracing his steps from there, his head down, examining every inch of the ground he covered.

Mary, her voice full of concern, said, "Down, Asinus. Let me down."

At first he was tempted to ignore her. Why should the two of them waste their time looking for something they weren't going to find? But of course they didn't know that, and since he couldn't tell them, he might as well let them satisfy themselves that their money was, in fact, gone. Lowering himself, he made it easy for Mary to step onto the ground. She hurried after her husband, helping him search for his lost purse.

While awaiting their return, Asinus began making new escape plans. It was more imperative than ever that he get away quickly because he was traveling with two people who no longer had two coins to rub together. How would they subsist in a strange town? They'd have to sell something. What did they have to sell? They had him and nothing else. But he did not intend to be sold again. Whoever bought him would not leave him untethered at night. He should already have taken advantage of this freedom Joseph gave him but, of course, through a series of fluke circumstances, the right moment had not yet come. He would have to make sure it came tonight.

When Joseph finally returned, empty-handed, with Mary at his side, he sat down on a stone bench and stared into space, obviously crestfallen, desolate and forlorn. She sat down beside him, put an arm around him and tried to comfort him.

"Don't worry, dear. We'll survive. Remember what you always say to me—God will provide."

There they go again with their "God will provide," Asinus said to himself, exasperated at their simplicity. Don't count on it today. This looks like God's day to provide for pickpockets.

Joseph shook his head sadly. "We haven't a mite to our name. I wish we'd run into that nice young man again. I'm sure he'd help us."

"Which nice young man?" Mary asked.

"The one who saved me from being hit by that donkey."

"How do you know he was so nice? Are you sure he doesn't have your purse?"

He looked aghast. "Mary, how can you think such things about people?"

"All I know," she said, "is that he's the only person who's touched you since the last time you had your purse in hand."

"I obviously dropped it," Joseph said. "It must have been right after I gave the coins to those poor beggars.

We're destitute in a strange town, and it's all my fault."

Mary said, "No, it's not."

And Asinus, when he stopped to think about it, had to agree. He knew enough about pickpockets to recognize that one as a real professional, an artist. He could lift anybody's purse. Maybe it was my fault, Asinus said to himself. I should have seen through it and stepped between them. And I shouldn't have been in such a hurry to get here. I knew the place was full of thieves. If we were still on the road, Joseph would still have his money.

A young man in a red-and-white-striped wollen tunic walked up and said to Joseph, "Aren't you the traveler who lost his purse?"

Joseph jumped to his feet, a hopeful expression on his face. "Yes, why? Did you find it? I'll give you a handsome reward."

"No, but I saw you searching for it."

"Oh."

"I was just wondering, it looks like you'll have to sell your donkey. How much do you want for him?"

Asinus said to himself, Here it comes. We'll see now how much he really cares about me after all his nice talk.

Joseph looked at the man as if he thought him insane. "Sell my donkey? Sell Asinus? I would as quickly sell myself."

When the young man went away, Mary threw her arms around Joseph and kissed him. "I was worried there for a moment," she said. "We've got nothing we could sell except Asinus. I was afraid you might be tempted. But I guess you really do believe God will provide."

"I also believe God helps those who help themselves," he said, "so I brought along some tools just in case I might have to do some carpentry. You see, my dear, I'm not as impractical as you think. Now let's go find an inn so you can rest while I look for work."

Though Joseph sounded almost lighthearted when he said this, he didn't fool Asinus. The man was simply trying to cheer up his wife. It wouldn't be easy for a carpenter from Nazareth to find work in a town like Shechem. The carpenters in Shechem would see to that. Joseph and Mary would need a much better solution to their troubles and Asinus found himself wishing now that he could think of one. He felt sheepish about Joseph's unexpected show of loyalty to him. It was not as unselfish as it looked. He was sure of that. Only if Joseph were desperate would he sell his donkey with his wife in her condition. And since he had brought along his tools, he apparently didn't yet feel desperate. But he would in a day or so when he discovered he couldn't find work. It was really sad. Even human beings didn't deserve this kind of fate. He should find some way to help them. He couldn't abandon them when they were in such deep trouble.

As they walked through the market streets in search of an inn, Asinus came up with what seemed like an appropriate idea out of his past. He would try a trick he had learned from a petty thief who had once owned him. It was a simple bit of larceny. But the circumstances had to be right.

They were approaching a dry goods shop when he noticed what looked like an ideal commodity for his purpose—expensive and negotiable. In the doorway of the shop were countless bolts of fine silk—red, green, blue, yellow and many other colors—stacked almost six cubits high. Walking past this costly display, he swished the side of his head into the pile about halfway between the top and bottom. The whole stack teetered momentarily, then, from the top, at least ten bolts of the precious cloth fell like a gift into Mary's lap as she sat in her saddle chair.

That ought to be enough at least to take care of their immediate problem, Asinus decided, walking nonchalantly on as if nothing had happened. It was important not to break into a run since that would attract attention. Even if Joseph had to sell it at cut prices on the street, he'd realize a tidy sum for ten or twelve bolts of silk.

Asinus was startled out of his reverie by Mary's voice. "Asinus! Stop! Joseph, stop him!" It was the first time Asinus had ever heard her raise her voice. And this was hardly the time for it. If she didn't shut up, everyone would notice that they were making off with the silk.

Joseph, who hadn't seen the silk fall into Mary's lap, grabbed Asinus's headstall and brought him to a stop. "What's the matter?" he said to Mary. "Where did you get all that cloth?"

"Asinus must have stumbled back there," she said. "He knocked it off the top of a pile in front of that shop."

"Asinus stumbled? He's so surefooted I didn't think he ever stumbled."

"Well, he must be dead tired. He's carried me a long way today."

Taking the bolts of cloth from Mary and stacking them in his arms, Joseph said, "This is a lot of silk. Wait here while I return it."

Return it! Asinus couldn't believe what he was hearing. Nobody had seen them take it. And the shopkeeper wouldn't miss it. He had a whole shopful of cloth. None of Asinus's previous owners would even have thought about returning it, especially if they were broke. And at the moment Joseph was destitute. There was no such thing as an honest man. Asinus knew that. But sometimes Joseph could almost make him think there was. As Joseph carried the silk bolts back to their rightful owner, Asinus watched with a mixture of anger, impatience, frustration, bewilderment and just a touch of wonder.

CHAPTER EIGHT

AFTER DIVESTING ASINUS OF THE SADDLE chair and the two heavy luggage packs, Joseph took hold of his headstall and led him down a gentle slope near the inn where he had installed Mary. Beside a small mountain stream at the bottom of this slope was the thickest patch of grass to be seen for miles around.

"Here's a nice meal for you," he said to the donkey. Asinus was puzzled at being led to pasture. Did the man think he was so dumb he couldn't find his way to grass? "But I'm afraid there'll be no barley for you today," Joseph continued, "and no warm stable to-night. I've lost all my money. Do you understand? No, of course not. How could you understand money? I'm not sure I understand it myself. If only I were a donkey. The grass, at least, is free. But Mary and I will have nothing to eat unless I can find work. And that might not be easy, though I wouldn't say it in front of her. So wish me luck, Asinus. There's still an hour or more before dark. I'd better start knocking on doors."

After Joseph left him, Asinus took only a few perfunctory nibbles at the good fresh grass. He didn't know why, but he just wasn't hungry. After a few more nibbles, he left the patch of grass and wandered toward the center of town, poking his head into each street and alley and occasionally into the open window of a house, as he walked. The place still looked fairly familiar to him. He had been at large for three days the time he escaped from the jute dealer. He remembered the square stone houses and he recognized the ruins of an ancient wall. Darkness was descending now. The streets were emptying rapidly and lamps were beginning to show in the windows.

He fell in beside the first donkey he saw, a big, friendly looking jack with a man on his back. "Good evening," Asinus said.

"If it doesn't rain."

"It doesn't look like rain."

"You never can tell."

"Feels too cold to rain."

"I don't know. I've been in some cold rains in my day."

Asinus said to himself, I must be getting soft-
headed. How did I get myself into this silly conversation? "I was wondering," he said, "do you by any
chance know a pickpocket in this town who uses the
galloping-donkey dodge?"

"Sorry," the other donkey said, "I'm a stranger here
myself."

Having wasted that much time, Asinus disengaged
himself and went down a wide street into a residential
area where, outside a large, two-story house, he saw a
tethered jénny with a saddle of the finest leather on
her back. She was an attractive, well-groomed gray,
though darker than himself. Apparently the property
of a wealthy family. "Good evening," he said to her.

She seemed not to hear him.

"I said, good evening."

Finally she turned her head. "Don't come near me,
you big brute."

"I only wanted to ask you . . ."

"I never speak to strangers."

Her snobbery annoyed him. "All right, don't speak
to me," he said. "You won't speak to another donkey
but you'll let a man ride your back. Talk to him and
see what he's got to say to you. Giddap and whoa and
a kick in the ribs if you go too slow." Turning from
her, he walked away in disgust.

"Wait!" she called after him. "Don't go. You're
rather attractive when you get mad."

He didn't look back. He couldn't stand donkeys who
were snooty because their owners were rich. In front
of an inn he saw another jenny who was at least willing

to talk to him. But when he asked her if she knew a pickpocket who used the donkey dodge, she said, "Why would I know a scoundrel like that? What kind of a donkey do you take me for?"

"I didn't mean to insult you," Asinus said. "We donkeys don't often get to decide who we'll associate with."

"Well, I don't associate with pickpockets," she said, "and I don't associate with donkeys who do, so you can just run along, Jack."

Giving up on that conversation, Asinus moved on to the town square, passing the very spot where Joseph had been robbed. Only a few people and a few donkeys were still in evidence. Most of the shops and peddlers' stalls were closed. He stopped next to a small donkey with a big pack on his back and asked about the pickpocket.

"I don't know him," this donkey said. "I don't live around here. But I saw him, all right. Clever devil. He extracted twenty shekels from the fellow who owns me."

"When?"

"About a half hour ago."

"Which way did he go?"

"That's what my owner would like to know. He's looking for him right now."

Asinus, somewhat encouraged, talked to another donkey and then another, but both of them were from out of town and couldn't help him. Finally he found a local, an old jack with a load of twigs on his back.

"Oh, you're talking about Asaph," he said. "You bet

I know him. See him around all the time. He's so well known everyone who lives here watches out for him. So he concentrates on travelers. Asaph's a legend in Shechem. Fastest hands in all Palestine, they say."

"That's the man," Asinus said. "How do I find him?"

"I don't know how a donkey would go about finding him," the old jack said, "but if you were a man, all you'd have to do is flash your money in public."

These words gave Asinus an idea. Maybe he should hang around a wineshop, where men were inclined to be free with their money. He set out to look for one, but before he had gone more than a block off the square, his attention was distracted by the sight of a man ahead of him in a gray cloak. Though the light was dim, he felt certain this was his quarry. The man moved with the same grace and quickness as the pickpocket he had seen that afternoon. Asinus broke into a trot to get closer and the man turned, hearing the donkey's footsteps. It was indeed Asaph. He had found the fellow at last. But to what avail?

He was still trying to work out a course of action when another man emerged from a nearby alley, saw Asaph and raced after him, shouting, "Thief! Thief! Stop that thief!"

Maybe this was the man from whom Asaph had lifted the twenty shekels. But when Asaph turned to find himself pursued, he didn't seem alarmed. There was no one on the street to stop him. Not deigning even to break into a run, he simply glided into another alley and disappeared. The man chasing him went plunging into the alley as if he had now cornered his prey, and Asinus went nosing in behind him, but even though the alley proved to be a dead end, it offered them no sign of Asaph. He seemed able to disappear as fast as he could make a man's purse disappear. It was almost dark now. Asinus finally gave up the search and returned to the patch of grass where Joseph had left him.

As he settled in for the night, he couldn't help feeling discouraged. Though he knew the name and face of the man for whom he was looking and was confident he could find him again, he still had no idea what to do when he did find him. His original plan of leading Joseph to him now seemed fatuous. There was no way to make Joseph realize the man had his money. Yet Asinus knew that as soon as morning came, he would set out once more to look for the clever pickpocket. Having once belonged to a pickpocket, he considered himself a connoisseur of the art. He was eager to follow Asaph and watch him operate, even if he couldn't get the better of him.

When Joseph came from the inn to the little brookside meadow to visit Asinus the next morning, his worries showed in his face. The cheerful smile and the usual ebullience were not there. The furrows in his brow seemed deeper than usual, the corners of his mouth were down. But his first words of concern were for the donkey.

"Are you getting enough to eat?" he asked, putting an arm around Asinus's neck. "Where did you sleep? Against that little embankment, I suppose. I hope you were warm enough. Thank God it wasn't cold or rainy. Anyway, I've got some good news for you. No heavy burdens and no long trek today. We're staying here. But I can't pretend that's good news for me. I've got to find a way to earn some money, Asinus, or I won't even be able to pay for our room at the inn. And the prospects aren't very good, I'm afraid. No luck last evening. I must have knocked on twenty doors. It was just before dusk, of course. Maybe I'll do better in broad daylight, but I'm not so sure. Nobody was very encouraging. I don't know what I'll do if Mary's time suddenly comes. I don't even know how I'll feed her when the few morsels in our knapsack are gone. I just don't know, but . . ." After another "Wish me luck," he went off once more, with a bagful of tools on his shoulder in search of work.

Asinus waited long enough to make certain Joseph was gone before he too left the little meadow, in search of Asaph, the pickpocket. He went first to the neighborhood in which he had caught a glimpse of him the night before, then to the town square, then up and down the streets around it, talking to one donkey after another. It was almost midday before a big roan in front of a wineshop said to Asinus, "You're wasting your time looking for Asaph in the morning. He's so good he doesn't have to work all day. I never see him until afternoon, when the town begins to fill up with travelers."

"That makes sense," Asinus admitted. "I should have realized it myself." The thing to do, he decided, was to put some food in his belly, then resume the search. "Where can a donkey steal a halfway decent meal around here?" he asked the roan.

"If you don't mind eating on the run," the roan said, "you can follow along behind some farmer and his donkey carrying grain to the market. All you have to do is bite a hole in a sack and it'll pour out faster than you can eat it."

Asinus, pursuing this advice, had just fallen in behind a donkey with two heavy grain sacks on his back and was about to take a bite out of the larger sack when, from the corner of his eye, he noticed Joseph trudging along the middle of the square, apparently still looking for work. Asinus's first reaction was a strange feeling he had never before experienced. He would be mortified, he suddenly realized, if Joseph were to see him stealing grain. But why? It was none of Joseph's business. It wouldn't even be necessary had Joseph known enough to hold onto his purse. If a man owned a donkey, he ought to be able to feed it, and if not, he could hardly blame the donkey for stealing enough to eat. When so many men were thieves, how could anyone blame an animal for taking just enough to survive? Yet for some reason, Asinus didn't like the thought of Joseph seeing him steal grain. It would be prudent, he decided, to get away from the square, at least while Joseph was there.

Still glancing back toward Joseph, he broke into a trot and ducked around the nearest corner, where he collided with two men who, at that moment, seemed to be brushing against each other. Unable to stop, he

sliced headlong between them with such force he sent both of them sprawling into the dirt. As he glanced back at them, the inelegance of their supine postures, and of the language each was directing toward him, persuaded him that his most prudent course was to continue on without slowing his pace. But just then he noticed on the ground between the two men a small leather purse.

At the same moment, one of the men also noticed the purse. Snatching it out of the dust with a lightning thrust of his hand, he broke off his vituperation against Asinus, leaped to his feet and disappeared into the gathering crowd.

Only then did Asinus realize that the man with the purse was Asaph, and that the collision with the elusive thief had happened just as he was picking the other man's pocket. Determined not to let Asaph get away this time, Asinus followed him into the crowd and, after apparently losing him again, finally spotted him hurrying away down a narrow street. Asinus quickened his pace in pursuit.

CHAPTER NINE

SAPH HAD EMERGED ONTO ANOTHER well-traveled street by the time Asinus closed in on him. There was no doubt he was the right man. He was still wearing his gray cloak and he was studying, with a pickpocket's concentration, two travelers just ahead of him. Asinus, exhilarated by his success in tracking down his quarry, began to wonder what he should do next. Though it was already mid-afternoon, and he had been straining for ideas since early morning, he still had no plan of action against the wily thief except to follow him, find out where he lived and somehow lead Joseph to him. Perhaps if Joseph were to talk to him he might eventually realize he was dealing with a thief. But wasn't that a vain hope? Joseph had so little evil in himself he never seemed to see it in other men.

On the other hand, Mary might catch on to Asaph. She was much more practical. Didn't she already harbor some suspicions? Hadn't she pointed out, right after Joseph was robbed, that the nice young man who had supposedly saved his life was the last person to touch him before his purse disappeared? Maybe that was the solution. Lead both Joseph and Mary to Asaph.

Meanwhile Asinus was eager to watch an artist like Asaph in action. Asinus had always admired and even envied pickpockets because they exemplified to him man's one superiority over animals. It must be wonderful, he thought, to have hands and to be able to use them so skillfully. He was quite convinced it was the hand, with its ability to grasp, to use tools and weapons, that enabled man to dominate the world. If he had hands, for instance, his problem with Asaph might be simplified. He would find out where the man kept his purse, then pick his pocket.

Asaph was now only a few feet behind his prospective victims. At any moment he should be creating some kind of distraction to put them off guard. Was his accomplice on the galloping donkey about to make another appearance? While Asinus dwelt on such speculations, Asaph simply moved up between the two men, said "Excuse me," and walked on ahead of them.

Asinus was puzzled. Surely Asaph hadn't scored that easily. From behind there had been no indication that his hands had even touched either man. Asinus stepped up his pace, moved ahead of the two men and followed Asaph at a prudent distance when he turned the next corner.

Walking quickly, Asaph had gone almost a half block before he glanced over his shoulder to make sure he wasn't followed by his victims. He then produced from someplace on his person not one but two purses. Asinus shook his head in wonder at the realization that he had robbed both men as he brushed past them. Dumping the contents of each purse into his left hand, Asaph, in almost the same motion, flung the two empty bags onto the flat roof of the building he was passing. That was good procedure, as Asinus had learned. If one of the town guards or one of your victims were to catch you, he wouldn't be able to identify the money on your person. One coin looked like another. But he might be able to identify a purse, so you had to get rid of that in a hurry.

From the right-hand pocket of his cloak, Asaph then produced a large leather purse into which he dumped the money he had stolen. As he was about to put this purse back into his cloak pocket, Asinus got another, closer look at it and, to his amazement, recognized it immediately as Joseph's. Perhaps Asaph was not such a perfectionist after all. Here, at least, was one purse he hadn't thrown away right after stealing it. Why not? Asinus wondered. No doubt because it was such a big one. Big enough to hold the proceeds of several more thefts.

Noticing that Asaph paid no attention to him, Asinus followed more closely as the pickpocket circled around and again entered the flow of traffic into the city. It was obvious that he concentrated on travelers. He fell in beside a merchant who was leading five donkeys, heavily laden with woolen cloth. Asinus pulled up close enough to hear the conversation.

"They tell me wine merchants drink the best wine," Asaph was saying to the man, "so it's only fitting that wool merchants should wear the best cloaks. That's a fine garment on your back, sir."

"No finer than yours," the merchant said.

"I only wish it were so," Asaph said, "but mine is a very poor piece of goods next to yours. A local product. The wool is only adequate. The stitching is crude, I fear. Here, let me show you my lining." He held his cloak open while the man examined it. "You see, yours is far superior. It would give me pleasure to examine it. Maybe then I could tell our local tailors how a real cloak is made."

It was as simple as that. Unfortunately for the wool merchant, he was charmed by Asaph's attention and flattery. A few minutes later, he was walking blithely through the square, not yet aware that Asaph, in a little side street, was discarding his empty purse. Once more, as Asinus watched, he put his loot into Joseph's purse, pulled the strings tight and returned the purse to his cloak pocket.

For an hour or more Asinus followed Asaph from one pickery to another, all executed with enviable skill. Some of his victims he would set up by engaging in conversation. Some he simply brushed against in passing. Some he would catch while they were haggling with peddlers or drawing water from the town well. He was even able to rob one man while the man was beating his donkey. Asinus enjoyed that. He became so charmed by Asaph's operations he almost forgot his own purpose in following the clever thief.

Asinus's attention was drawn back to his purpose when, after one of Asaph's money transfers, he returned Joseph's purse somewhat carelessly to his cloak pocket so that its strings dangled outside. Asinus felt his pulse quicken. He saw immediately the opportunity offered by this surprising mistake. Even without hands he now had a chance to pick a pickpocket's pocket. What a coup that would be.

They were walking through the marketplace and approaching a corner. Right at the corner was a fruit peddler's cart. Coming up beside it, just two or three paces behind Asaph, Asinus swung his hindquarters into the cart, knocking it over and dumping its contents onto the ground. A moment later, oranges, lemons, grapes, figs and pomegranates were rolling in every direction. The peddler shrieked and all heads turned, including Asaph's. Gleefully, and perhaps with just a bit of larceny in mind, he joined other

passersby in gathering up the fruit. Asinus waited until Asaph was down on one knee, filling his arms with oranges, then, stepping up carefully behind him, took the strings of Joseph's purse between his teeth. With utmost delicacy he lifted the heavy leather pouch from the man's cloak pocket. Everybody was having so much fun retrieving fruit that no one noticed the big gray-white donkey trotting away with his precious mouthful. He and Joseph were even now. Tonight he would make his escape at last, and no one could ever say he had deserted the man when he was down. Joseph would soon have twice as much money as he had lost. He could easily buy another donkey and continue his journey as if he had never been robbed.

Returning to the inn, Asinus wondered how best to get the money to Joseph and Mary before he left them. He was walking around the building, trying to figure out which room was theirs, when he heard Joseph's voice through an open window. Poking his head into the window, he saw the two of them, by the light of a lamp, sitting on straw beds near the far corner. Joseph looked dejected.

"I want you to eat," he was saying to Mary.

"I've had more than enough," she said. "You must eat something yourself."

"I told you I had some bread this afternoon."

"Joseph, you're a good carpenter," she said, "and a wonderful husband, but a completely incompetent liar."

"Well, I'm not hungry," he insisted.

Mary reached for his hand. "I wish I could relieve your worries, dear. I feel like a burdèn on you."

"Don't say such a thing."

"Do you still think you'll be able to get someone here to hire you?"

"I'll have better luck tomorrow," he assured her.

"And if not?"

"Then I'll think of something else to do. Don't worry, darling. God will provide."

Asinus was exasperated at hearing again this oft-repeated prayer. How come their God got all the credit when their donkey did all the work? Dropping the purse out of his mouth onto the floor of the room, he turned to walk away.

Joseph, hearing a noise near the window, came over to it, looked out, and, despite the darkness, caught sight of the donkey.

"Asinus!" he called.

Disappearing from the window, he quickly emerged from the inn, caught up to Asinus and took hold of him gently by the headstall.

"Where were you?" he cried. "I went down the hill looking for you a few minutes ago and couldn't find you. But I knew you wouldn't wander far. Come on, old fellow, I'll walk back down there with you and pull up some tall grass for you. Make you a nice soft bed."

If you had any sense, Asinus thought to himself, you'd go back into that room and find your purse. He was annoyed at Joseph for coming out and making this fuss over him. Though the man didn't know it, they were now through with each other. Why didn't he go back inside to his wife and stop showing off with all this embarrassing kindness? Asinus was ready to concede now that Joseph wasn't a bad man, but he himself hadn't treated Joseph badly, so they were even. Why couldn't Joseph leave it at that?

It was too much to hope. When they reached the little meadow beside the brook, Joseph went right to work, gathering long reeds of grass by the armful and making a bed of it, up against the sheltered embankment where Asinus had slept the previous night. "This isn't much of a bed," he said, "but it's the best I can offer you tonight. And I don't know what I can do for you tomorrow, Asinus, if I don't earn some money. They may put me in prison if they find out I can't pay my bill at the inn. My only hope is that Ichabod, Jabez and Caleb catch up to us soon. They might loan me enough to get back to Nazareth, though I don't know why they should. I wasn't very helpful to them when they needed me."

Asinus shuddered at the very mention of those three names. How long, he wondered, will the man carry on like this? I don't want his bed. I don't plan to sleep here tonight. Will he never leave me alone so I can grab a few bites of grass and be on my way?

It occurred to Asinus that he hadn't eaten anything since early morning. That was why he was so hungry. But he was also tired to the point of exhaustion. It had been a long, busy day.

"There you are," Joseph said as he patted the grass mattress into place. "An all-purpose bed. You can sleep on it tonight and eat it in the morning."

Asinus opened his mouth wide and did an imitation of a human yawn. He had observed that whenever a man yawned, people around him were likely to do the same. Maybe if he were to yawn often enough, Joseph would start yawning and get sleepy. He yawned again and again and again.

Finally Joseph yawned. Asinus yawned once more, and so did Joseph. "You must be tired," he said to Asinus. "I'm getting sleepy myself. I'll leave you now but I'll be back at dawn."

Asinus was astonished at his success. If he had known yawning worked that well on people, he'd have tried it long ago in the middle of the day. He began eating the grass bed Joseph had gathered for him. It was easier than feeling for grass in the dark. And he had no need for it as a bed since he'd be leaving in a few minutes. But he was awfully tired. He couldn't deny that. He wouldn't get very far tonight without at least a short rest. Maybe he should take a little nap before leaving. It would do him good. He lay down on the pad of grass, stretched his legs and closed his eyes.

CHAPTER TEN

 SINUS! WHERE ARE YOU?"

Waking to the sound of Joseph's distant voice, Asinus opened his eyes in bewilderment to find that it was after dawn. He had slept the night away, wasting still another opportunity to escape. Frustrated and furious at himself, he leaped to his feet and looked around in all directions, trying to convince himself it wasn't so.

Joseph, with his bag of carpentry tools again slung from his shoulder, came down the hill and approached him. "I do believe you were sleeping," he said. "Sorry if I woke you. I just wànted to say hello. Go back to sleep. There's nothing else to do. We can't get away from here until I earn some money."

Money! Was it possible he had spent the whole night in that room, then got up and got dressed there this morning, without once noticing his big fat purse on the floor? He never seemed to notice anything, yet he could walk through one perilous situation after another unscathed. He could stay dry in a downpour. If the sky were to fall, it would miss him. But now, for a change, Joseph's detachment and oversight might operate in Asinus's favor. With Joseph gone until nightfall looking for work, Asinus would have plenty of time to escape unnoticed, even though it was broad daylight.

Despite his impatience, he stood still while Joseph fussed over him as usual, currying his coat and cleaning the mud from his hooves. The man had just begun examining his teeth when Mary appeared at the top of the hill, waving something in her hand. He seemed not to comprehend what it was until she came down the hill and handed it to him.

"Look what I found!" she cried.

"That's my purse!" he exclaimed.

"Indeed it is," she said, "with all your money in it and then some. And do you know where I found it? Right in our room, by the window, as if someone had reached in and dropped it there. Something peculiar is going on around here, Joseph. Only Asinus was near that window last night."

With trembling fingers Joseph loosened the strings and opened the purse. When he looked into it, his eyes widened. "I don't understand it," he gasped. "There's much more money here than I lost. It looks like twice as much. Tell me exactly, now, where did you find it?"

"On the floor, directly below the window."

"But that's where I put our donkey packs."

"It was right next to them."

"Well, that explains everything," Joseph said. "I must have put my purse in one of the packs just after I gave the coins to those three beggars."

"Why would you have done that?"

"I don't know, darling. I don't even remember doing it but sometimes I can be absentminded. Have you never noticed?"

She smiled benevolently. "It has occurred to me. But if that's what happened, where did all this extra money come from? Have we got a money tree in one of those packs?"

"There's only one possible explanation," Joseph said. "The extra money is a gift from God."

"It is that," Mary agreed. "With a child coming we'll need every bit of it."

After they recovered from the excitement of finding themselves suddenly with so much money, Joseph paid the innkeeper and they were soon on the road once more, still hoping to make Jerusalem before the Sabbath. They had been traveling about an hour and were trudging slowly up another of the many steep hills along their route, when Joseph turned to Mary and said, "I only hope your time doesn't come while we're climbing these mountains."

Asinus could understand Joseph's concern. Mary looked pale and drawn this morning, as well she might after a day and a half of apparent destitution in a strange town, and she also looked as if she might be ready to deliver at any moment. Yet she didn't seem worried about it. "The child will not be born," she said, "until we reach Bethlehem."

She must know more about such things than I do, Asinus decided. He had thought babies came when they were ready, not when their mothers were ready for them. But with Mary he wasn't so sure. She had a strong will beneath her gentle exterior.

Joseph hoped by nightfall, he said, to reach the holy city of Bethel, which Jacob, in the Scriptures, had called the House of God and the Gate of Heaven. But it would be a hard day's journey since the entire route was mountainous. After their late start, they had traveled less than halfway by midday. They stopped only long enough for Asinus to eat a bag of grain, and themselves half a loaf of bread with some olives.

It was midafternoon and they were approaching the top of a hill when Joseph happened to look back and see, about a half mile behind them, three men riding three donkeys.

"I believe those are our friends," he said. "We should stop and wait for them."

Mary and Asinus also turned. There was no doubt in Asinus's mind: the three men were Ichabod, Jabez and Caleb, and they were whipping their donkeys to hurry them along. Asinus decided he had better hurry himself along. He did not want to be caught by those three in these hills. There were too many lonely, isolated places in the miles ahead where they could easily carry out the murderous plot he had managed to thwart two days earlier. He had no plan in mind for thwarting it again, except to stay ahead of them. But that wouldn't be easy because, although their three donkeys could never catch him, they would eventually catch Joseph.

While he was considering the dismal prospects, Mary said to Joseph, "I don't think we dare wait for them, dear, if you want to make Bethel before dark."

"We'll get there," he assured her. "We still have plenty of time."

"But have you looked at the sky? Those are dark clouds ahead. I think we're in for a bad storm."

"God will protect us," Joseph said.

"Don't you think He has other things to do? If we can save ourselves from a storm, He'll hardly be pleased to see us depend on Him."

"Neither will He be pleased if we ignore our friends."

"But I don't believe they are our friends, Joseph."

"I want to prove to you that they are," he said. "It saddens me that you look upon them with suspicion after they've been so kind to us. And it embarrasses me that I did nothing to help them when those rocks fell."

"You might be right," she said, "but I still don't trust them."

"Do you trust me?"

"Of course."

"Then just relax, my darling, and let me handle things."

"All right, dear, if you say so."

"You can stop now, Asinus," Joseph called to the donkey.

Mary, after heaving a sigh, sat back in her saddle chair and seemed to relax, but a moment later, as Asinus was about to break into a run because he could think of nothing else to do, he was astonished to feel her sandals poking surreptitiously against his flanks. She was actually telling him to run. Joyously he bounded forward, just as Joseph was about to take hold of his headstall. They were ten cubits away by the time Joseph recovered from his surprise. "Stop!" he cried.

"Not too fast," Mary whispered in Asinus's ear. "Just fast enough to keep him coming. Maybe we can catch up to someone else before those three catch up to us."

Though it was their only hope, Asinus began to despair of it happening as he ran up one hill and down another with Joseph close behind him, begging the donkey to stop. If Asinus had wanted the road to himself, he would surely have found it crowded, but now that he wanted company, there seemed to be no traffic at all. Except for Ichabod, Jabez and Caleb. Each time he glanced over his shoulder he saw them coming closer as they whipped their donkeys up to top speed. They were so close now that Ichabod could be heard shouting at Joseph to stop.

"I will if I can catch my donkey," Joseph shouted back.

As they approached the top of still another steep and craggy rise, with Joseph obviously tiring and their pursuers less than a quarter of a mile behind them, Asinus began to abandon hope. But when he reached the crest of this hill, he saw in a narrow valley ahead of them a caravan of donkeys going their way. If they could attach themselves to that caravan before they were caught, they might have at least some protection. It would be easy for Asinus to overtake the caravan in time, but could Joseph make it? Fortunately the race was downhill. Asinus increased his pace slightly, forcing Joseph to maximum speed. Even so, they had gone only two hundred cubits down the slope when their pursuers reached the crest behind them. They were gaining fast. At the same time, Asinus, Mary and Joseph were getting closer to the caravan. Now, however, there was a new worry. The donkeys ahead were making a turn around the edge of another hill, which would put them out of sight until Asinus, Mary and Joseph made the same turn. If Ichabod, Jabez and Caleb were to catch them while they were out of sight of the caravan, Mary wouldn't be able even to shout for help. With this in mind, Asinus fixed his eyes on that turn in the road as the caravan disappeared around it.

They still had four hundred cubits to go with their

pursuers only a hundred behind them. Then three hundred, two hundred, one hundred to go with the three men only twenty-five behind them and shouting at them to stop. Joseph, too, while keeping pace with Asinus, was still shouting at him to stop as they came within fifty, then twenty-five cubits of the turn in the road. When Asinus reached the turn and followed it to the left, their pursuers were only a few cubits behind them, but at the same time, the caravan was within shouting distance ahead.

Ichabod, riding Hepzibah, came abreast of Joseph and said to him, "Don't worry, I'll catch that infernal runaway for you." And Asinus allowed Ichabod to do so, but not until he had caught up to the caravan, whose leader, out of curiosity, had stopped his donkeys.

Asinus was standing still, firmly in Ichabod's grasp, when Joseph, Jabez and Caleb finally overtook them. Joseph's first concern was for Mary, but as soon as she assured him she was unharmed, he turned to Ichabod.

"Once again I owe you a debt of gratitude," he said. "I don't know what I'd have done if you hadn't come along to stop my donkey. He's a marvelous beast, but sometimes he gets it into his head to run and there's no stopping him."

"I think the beast abuses you grievously," Ichabod said, "but as for your kind words about me, you owe me nothing."

"I can't thank you enough," Joseph said. "I couldn't have kept pace with Asinus much longer."

"Asinus, you say! I thought I recognized that monster!"

The voice of the caravan master had suddenly broken into the conversation—a loud, rasping voice that made Asinus shudder. When Asinus turned toward him, he was looking into a familiar though not a friendly face. This was the rug dealer from Bethlehem who had once owned him, a man named Phineas who had the voice of a jackal and the disposition of a weasel. He sold rugs that he claimed were "from the Orient" but which in fact were woven by poor, underpaid women in a Bethlehem barn.

Joseph turned to him with a puzzled expression. "You mean you recognize my donkey?"

"Brother, if that's your donkey," Phineas said, "you got troubles. I know. I owned him once myself."

"But he's a wonderful creature," Joseph said. "He's never given me any trouble."

Ichabod said, "He just ran away from you, didn't he!"

"Not really," Joseph corrected. "If he'd wanted to run away, he'd be miles down the road by now. He's a very fast donkey."

"I'll give you that," said Phineas. "He ran away from me and he was a very devil to catch. If I had more sense I'd have let him go, but I paid too much for him. A crooked, conniving jute dealer sold him to me in Shechem a year or two ago for an outrageous price."

That's right, Asinus recalled. Seven shekels. And you unloaded me to that wine merchant for nine.

"I could tell you stories about this donkey," Phineas continued in his belligerent, grating voice. "The first time I put a pack on his back he threw it over the side of a cliff. Five precious rugs and I lost every one of them."

It wasn't just the first time you put a pack on my back, Asinus recalled. It was also the last time. And those rugs were rags.

"I'm sorry for your loss," Joseph said, "but I don't understand. It must have been an accident. He likes to run sometimes, I'll admit. Yet he's carried my wife all the way from Nazareth and it's been the smoothest of rides, has it not, my dear?"

"Surely the world has never seen a more gentle donkey," Mary said, whereupon she was greeted by derisive laughter from Ichabod, Jabez, Caleb and Phineas.

"I'm glad he's yours now and not mine," Phineas said. "You're welcome to him."

"I think we should be getting on," Ichabod said to Joseph. "Those clouds ahead look ominous."

Mary said, "Why don't we travel with this caravan?"

"It would be too slow," Ichabod pointed out. "We can make much better time on our own. It looks as if there's a big storm brewing and I don't want you to get soaked."

"That's very kind of you," she replied, "but I doubt if there's any rain in those clouds."

Joseph looked startled. "My darling, you said yourself a while ago you thought we were in for a downpour. And the clouds are darker now than they were then. I think you should leave the matter up to me. I don't want you to be drenched."

The matter was, of necessity, left up to Asinus, who refused to move on ahead of the caravan when they got underway. Ichabod, Jabez and Caleb, apparently eager to leave the caravan in the dust, pulled out at a rapid walk, expecting Joseph, Mary and Asinus to follow, and indeed Joseph did keep pace with them until he noticed that Asinus was lagging behind.

"Come along, Asinus," he called over his shoulder, "or we'll lose our friends."

Mary, with a hand behind her back, patted his flank lightly, as if to say, Pay no attention.

Ichabod, confronted with this latest of Asinus's quirks, could hardly contain his exasperation. "What's the matter with that animal?" he cried. "A minute ago you couldn't stop him. Now you can't get him started."

Joseph said, "I'm afraid he's tired after his run."

Asinus, ignoring both of them, simply kept pace with the donkey train. Though he would hardly choose Phineas as a traveling companion under ordinary circumstances, he was quite eager to stay with him for the rest of this day.

Joseph and Ichabod waited for Asinus to come abreast of them. Joseph patted his shoulder and said, "You can do better than that, old boy. Speed up a little."

When Asinus failed to respond, Ichabod said, "You

know, I hate to see anyone strike an animal. I deplore violence. But with this donkey of yours, I'm afraid strong measures are necessary."

Joseph was astonished. "Are you suggesting I take a stick to him?"

"Not you," Ichabod said. "You and I are too gentle for that sort of thing. But I notice that Phineas carries a very persuasive whip. I'm sure he could influence the beast."

"It'd be a pleasure," Phineas bellowed, "to give that demon a few good whacks."

"Never!" cried Joseph. "I know that some men whip their animals, but no man will whip mine."

"I feel the same way myself," Ichabod said, "but I was worried about your wife if the rain should begin."

Mary said, "You can both stop worrying about me. It'll take more than raindrops to wash me away."

Joseph and Ichabod, shrugging in resignation, walked along beside Asinus, who continued to keep pace with the twenty or more donkeys in Phineas's caravan.

After they had gone a distance in silence, Joseph said to Ichabod, "I'm afraid I owe you an apology."

"Why so?"

"For not staying to help you after the rockslide."

"That wasn't your fault. That was your donkey's fault. You had to chase him."

"I felt bad about it, nevertheless."

Ichabod put a hand on his shoulder. "It warms my heart," he said, "to meet a man like you."

"How so?"

"In these modern times, it reaffirms my faith to find one who shares it with me."

"Why should we not share our faith?" Joseph asked.

"Why not indeed," Ichabod said, "but there are woefully many who have lost it. Our streets and highways are full of crime, and Godlessness is everywhere. It makes me want to cry out with the Prophet: 'Lord, how long shall the wicked, how long shall the wicked triumph? They break in pieces thy people, O Lord, and afflict thine heritage. They slay the widow and the stranger, and murder the fatherless.' "

"But didn't the same prophet say, 'Judgment shall return unto righteousness: and all the upright in heart shall follow it'?"

"When?" said Ichabod. "When shall we return to righteousness? We are still, in the words of Isaiah, 'a sinful nation, a people laden with iniquity.' "

"How do you come to be so learned in the Scriptures?" Joseph asked.

"Me? You call me learned? You do me too great an honor, my friend. But what I know, I learned at my father's knee. And if I know it well, give him the credit, for he was a very strict, exacting father, and he demanded all good things of me."

"It seems to me you've well fulfilled his demands."

"I hope so, but I don't claim it."

Asinus became so disgusted listening to this that he turned his mind from it and struck up a conversation with one of Phineas's donkeys, a scraggly roan jack whose ribs showed through his hide. "You look as if Phineas is still saving money on feed," he said to the jack. "How often do you get a full meal?"

"Only when he puts us out to pasture between trips. He doesn't even let us forage at night for fear we'll run away. Are you the Asinus I've heard other donkeys talk about?"

"I don't know. What do they say?"

"They say you make trouble for your owners."

"I try to," Asinus said, "but I never seem to get anyplace. All my life I've been telling donkeys to rebel against people, but they pay no attention to me."

"You've got fertile ground here," the jack said. "Every one of us would like to rebel against Phineas."

"How long have you been with him?"

"Long enough to lose about thirty pounds. Three or four months."

Asinus looked up and down the line of donkeys without seeing one he recognized. All of them were thin and undernourished. "Phineas has really got his system perfected, hasn't he?"

"What system?"

"You mean you've been with him three months and you don't yet know what he's doing to you? He figured out long ago that by giving his donkeys half-portions of feed, he could save enough money before they wore out to pay for their replacements."

"He gives us half-portions, all right," the roan jack said, "but I always thought it was just because he's so stingy. It's hard to believe that even a man like Phineas would be that cold and calculating. It's inhuman."

"On the contrary," Asinus said, "it's very human. Even men who feed us well get rid of us when we're no longer useful. Phineas is just a little more efficient than most men. He starves his donkeys because it's cheaper to replace them than feed them."

"You know, you may be right," the roan jack said. "Whenever a donkey gets too weak to carry a load, Phineas says, 'I know somebody who'll buy you,' and leads him away. Then he comes back with a healthy new donkey to replace him. But how many people can he possibly know who'll buy starving donkeys?"

"Now do you see why you ought to revolt? Look at the other donkeys in your train. Some of them are even skinnier than you are."

Just then Asinus heard a whip crack and saw its hideous tip bite into the hindquarters of the donkey to whom he was talking. The unfortunate creature, distracted by his conversation with Asinus, had fallen back a few paces. Phineas, now walking at the rear of the train, had used on him a whip Asinus remembered all too well, a vicious instrument that carried enough sting to make a bull jump.

Accompanying the whip, and sounding downright evil, came Phineas's brassy voice: "Get up there where you belong, you lazy rascal!"

It was enough to end the discussion between the two donkeys. The strange conglomeration of travelers walked on in silence, up one rise and down another, as the clouds ahead became ever more ominous. Bolts of lightning began to flash; thunder roared and heavy, oppressive, fearsome clouds brought semidarkness before its hour. Finally the first shower of cold rain fell in big drops, increasing from moment to moment until a steady downpour was soaking men and beasts.

Joseph, at the first sprinkles, threw his own cloak over Mary's shoulders, ignoring her protest that she didn't need it. "I'm afraid this is only the beginning," he said. "We'll be well and truly soaked before we reach Bethel."

"We'd be in Bethel already," Ichabod reminded him, "if that donkey of yours weren't so stubborn. Even now we could save ourselves some misery by pressing on ahead of this caravan."

Asinus, ignoring his words as well as the rain, held steady with the pace of the donkey train. By the time they did reach Bethel, shortly before nightfall, they were all so wet the continuing cloudburst could inflict no further miseries upon them. The sky had opened up now, bellowing its proud thunder and showing off its electric spectacle as it poured sheets and sheets of water on the already sodden earth. The men and donkeys had to walk through streams, then roaring rivulets of water as they made their way along the narrow valley to the gate of Bethel and up its now-deserted main street.

It was fortunate that they were with Phineas because he knew the town well and led them directly to a large inn with a stable attached. Though he had no intention of stabling his own donkeys, he was quite gracious about accommodating Joseph, who insisted on finding a place to shelter Asinus from the driving rain. Ichabod, Jabez and Caleb, perhaps shamed by Joseph, decided to do likewise for their donkeys, but when they entered the stable and reached for their purses to pay the groom, Jabez and Caleb found themselves suddenly astounded, alarmed, embarrassed and infuriated. Their purses were gone.

"My money!" Caleb gasped, digging into his pocket.

"We been robbed!" Jabez shouted, searching his person.

Joseph looked at them in disbelief. "Robbed? Surely not. No doubt you've misplaced your purses. You'll find them soon enough."

"We been robbed, I tell you," Jabez repeated. "I oughta know a robbery when I see it."

"While we were in Shechem," Joseph said, "I was beginning to think I might have been robbed. For a whole day or more I couldn't find my purse, but it turned out that I had simply misplaced it."

Ichabod said, "Shechem! That's where it happened. It was that young fellow in the gray cloak. I thought he was too slick. I kept my distance from him. You two should have done the same."

"How strange," Joseph said. "I also met a young man there in a gray cloak, but he was no thief. He couldn't have been nicer to me."

Asinus, unable to contain his mirth, began to laugh out loud. The three donkeys of Ichabod, Jabez and Caleb stared at him balefully. Until this moment, they hadn't had a chance to speak to him since their reunion.

Amos said to him, "What are you laughing at, Asinus? If these fellows have no money, we'll be out in the rain all night."

"That's not what I'm laughing at," Asinus said. But how could he explain to them what had happened in Shechem and the exquisite irony of Asaph, the ace of pickpockets, losing all that money to the innocent Joseph, then getting some of it back from the unscrupulous Jabez and Caleb? "Don't worry," he assured the three donkeys, "you won't be put out in the rain. My man Joseph loves to scatter his money. If I know him, he'll pay to keep you here."

Aaron said, "Do you know how much trouble you've caused us, Asinus? Thanks to you and your rockslide, we spent a frigid night, plus half the next day, on that mountain ledge."

"Sorry about that," Asinus said, "but I had to do something. Your friends were about to kill us."

Hepzibah said to Asinus, "You wouldn't laugh so hard if you could hear Ichabod talk about you. He saw you kick the boulder out from under the pile. He figures he'd have had Joseph's money long ago if it hadn't been for you. Now he's absolutely determined to kill you, and he loves to kill. I can tell you that."

"Thanks a lot," Asinus said, "but what can I do about him?"

"Listen, if I knew what to do about Ichabod," she said, "I wouldn't be here."

Jabez and Caleb were still fuming at the loss of their purses. Joseph tried to comfort them. "Did not the Prophet Isaiah tell us, 'He that hath no money; come ye, buy and eat; yea, come, buy wine and milk without money and without price.' "

Caleb was not comforted. "I'd like to see your friend Isaiah tell that to a wine merchant."

"My dear man, if you have faith," Joseph said, "your money will be returned to you tenfold. Or at least twofold. Take me, for example. I was desolate when I lost my purse in Shechem. But when I recovered it, look what I found." Reaching into his cloak, he brought forth the bulging pouch. "Would you believe this? Twice as much money as I had lost. It could only be a gift from God. So you see it pays to have faith. Here, let me share my good fortune with you." Extracting a handful of coins, he divided them roughly without counting them and gave half each to Jabez and Caleb. "It will tide you over, at least, until you find your purses. Now I must go and attend my wife. I don't want her to catch cold."

As Joseph returned to his room in the inn, the eyes of the three scoundrels were bulging almost as much as the carpenter's purse. When they were alone, Jabez looked around to make certain the stableman was out of earshot, then said to Caleb, "Did I just see what I just saw?"

Caleb put one of Joseph's gift coins between his teeth and bit it. "Feels real enough," he said. "But where could he have got hold of all that money?"

"I don't care where he got it," Ichabod said. "The question is, how do we get it? I'm tired of chasing the silly fool. We've let him slip through our fingers for the last time."

Jabez said, "He's smarter'n I thought he was."

"He's not smart at all," Ichabod corrected. "It's that wife of his, and that donkey. We've got to get rid of both of them. And we start with the donkey. Tonight."

Walking up to Asinus's stall, he said with venom in his voice, "I know how Balaam felt. 'Because thou hast mocked me, I would there were a sword in mine hand, for now would I kill thee.' "

Jabez took from his belt one of the many daggers he carried and offered it to Ichabod. "No sooner said than done."

Ichabod said, "Put that knife away, you impenetrable blockhead. Do you want the stableman to see us? This isn't the place to kill the infernal beast."

"Where then?"

"Later tonight, after everyone is asleep, we'll come back and take him out to where the caravan donkeys are tethered. Then when the carcass is found in the morning, Joseph will blame that loudmouthed rug merchant. Didn't the fellow say this afternoon, in front of all of us, that he hated the beast?"

Four hours later, when the only sound in the stable was the unceasing downpour of rain upon the roof and the repeated crashes of thunder, the door creaked open and Ichabod poked his head inside to make sure the stableman was no longer up and about. Satisfied that the way was clear, Ichabod tiptoed inside with Jabez and Caleb behind him. They were fortunate that the rain was making so much noise because the whispers of Jabez and Caleb were almost as loud as the talk of other men. And Caleb was so clumsy he stumbled several times, to the accompaniment of angry oaths, as they felt their way through the dark barn. They went directly to the stall Asinus had been occupying when they left him. Alas for them, he was not there.

Anticipating their arrival but unable to get out of the stable (again he decried his lack of hands), he had stationed himself behind a pile of hay near the bolted door. Now that they had opened the door, he was able to slip through it. But not unnoticed. At the moment of his escape, a great streak of lightning lit up the sky and the earth. Ichabod, finding Asinus's stall empty, turned just in time to see him, by this great light, running out the open door.

"There he goes!" Ichabod cried. "After him!"

The rain was falling in such horrendous volume that Asinus, emerging into it, was momentarily blinded by it. Before he could find his bearings and choose a direction in which to run, Caleb had also emerged from the stable, scourge in hand. Demonstrating his unquestionable skill with a whip, he lashed out and coiled the end of it around the donkey's left hind leg. But he had not reckoned with the animal's size and strength. At the sting of the whip, Asinus bolted forward, pulling Caleb off his feet, landing him in the mud and dragging him several cubits before the man let go of the whip. Accustoming himself to the rain, Asinus continued on at top speed, chased by the three men and dragging the whip for some distance before he dared slow up enough to let it uncoil. He was pleased to have disarmed Caleb, but he would have to watch out for Jabez, who had all those daggers to throw.

Asinus had one significant advantage over the three men as he ran through the streets and alleys of Bethel. He knew the town, probably better than they did. He also had some other advantages—his speed, the darkness and the obscurity provided by the enveloping rain—but these were offset by the small size of the town. He had little space in which to maneuver and they could cut him off before he could reach the city gate.

Though the chase began as a pell-mell footrace, after Asinus outran the men so they could no longer see him through the watery gloom, it became a silent, stealthy hunt in which they stalked him from one end of town to the other. They split up now so that as he made his way quietly and carefully from place to place, he never knew when one of them might pop out at him. He remembered a cave on a hillside where he would be relatively safe if he could reach it unseen, but he didn't dare go to it unless he had shaken them; if they were to follow him there they would have him trapped.

Feeling exposed and perilously vulnerable on the streets, he tried to stick to the alleys, though he felt by no means safe even there because one of the men might be lurking in any doorway or behind any pile of refuse. He was jittery and chilled as much by fear as by the cold rain. He entered one alley, stepping lightly to make as little noise as possible, and was greeted by unidentifiable sounds not more than twenty cubits ahead. Should he back away? Before he had time to decide, he caught sight of two figures racing toward him. Bracing himself, he raised a front leg, at the same time aware of what an inadequate weapon it was. No matter. He would fight them with whatever he had. But instead of attacking, they ran past him. He had disturbed two jackals eating garbage.

In another alley he heard the distinct sound of a man's footsteps approaching. There was no time to back away. He had to continue on toward the footsteps, hoping to come upon a pile of junk to hide behind. But the sound of the man was coming closer and closer. Asinus was about to despair when he saw through the sheets of rain something even better than a pile of junk. It was a stable door, wide open. He ducked inside just before the man passed. Despite the darkness, Asinus could see the silhouette of a raised arm and a flash of metal. Perhaps a knife blade. The man was tall and thin—exactly the size of Jabez.

Peering out of still another alley, he saw another man a good distance down the street, but this could not be one of his three pursuers. He was carrying a lamp, which explained why he could be seen at such a distance. Probably one of the town guards making his rounds. If he were to find Ichabod, Jabez and Caleb abroad at this time of night, he might arrest them as prowlers. But how could a donkey lead him to them, especially when he didn't even know where they were? He was still thinking idly about this when someone from behind grabbed his headstall.

A voice recognizable as Ichabod's cried out: "Gotcha!"

Asinus brayed in fright as well as anger and reared. He swung his head savagely from side to side, trying to break Ichabod's hold. Then he sprang sideways at a nearby wall with all his strength and weight, banging the man brutally against the wall, but Ichabod still clung to his harness.

"Jabez! Caleb!" he shouted desperately. "I've got him! Help me!"

Since Ichabod was short and slender, Asinus was able to buffet and scrape him against the side of the building, making him gasp and cry out even more urgently for help, but the man still would not let go. Deciding on a new strategy, Asinus began running down the street, dragging Ichabod behind him, but Ichabod was nimble and clever. By a heroic effort he managed to push off the ground with his right foot and swing himself up onto the donkey's back. Wrapping his arms around Asinus's neck, he held on with all his strength as Asinus galloped and turned and twisted. Within a few minutes he found himself running along the bank of a stream which, thanks to the flooding rains, was now a raging torrent.

"Caleb! Jabez!" Ichabod kept shouting, "where are you!"

At any moment, one or both of them was certain to

appear, making it almost impossible for Asinus to escape. If he wanted to save himself, he would have to do something other than running aimlessly along this swollen stream.

Swinging away from it, he raced up a hilly street perpendicular to it. At the top of the street, he turned around and, gathering speed as he descended, ran straight for the water's edge.

Ichabod, sensing the donkey's intention, clung desperately to his neck and emitted a ghastly scream.

As Asinus approached the bank at full speed, he lowered his head and neck as far as possible, thus drawing Ichabod farther forward. Then he sprang into the air with a mighty leap, put his four legs out in front, stiffened them, and braced them, and came down on all of them at once. Of the many sudden stops he had inflicted on men who had tried to ride him, this was the suddenest.

Ichabod, screeching hideously, somersaulted head over heels into the roaring maelstrom.

Asinus's first impulse was to run, but then he looked over the bank and was able, though barely, to see Ichabod clinging to something in the water as he continued his shouts for help. Jabez and Caleb were certain to show up soon. Maybe it would be worthwhile waiting for them.

Moments later, as Asinus concealed himself at the side of a nearby house, Caleb came running to the bank of the stream, easily identifiable not only by the outline of his stocky bulk but by his wheezing voice. "Ichabod!" he cried. "That you down there?"

"Where do you think I am?" Ichabod shouted back. "In Solomon's Temple?"

"What you doin' in the water?"

"Stop yapping, you idiot, and come down here. The water's running so fast I don't dare let go of this branch."

Since Ichabod was so eager to have Caleb down there with him, Asinus decided he should help Caleb get there. He wished suddenly that he were a goat. He envied goats their horns because with horns one could be more effective than with hooves. While it was true that kicking could be more forceful, more explosive, he had to admit that butting was more accurate because you could look right at the person you were butting, whereas if you wanted to kick with any power, you had to kick with your hind legs, either sensing the location of your target, or looking over your shoulder, which could throw off your aim. He wondered if he should try butting Caleb. It was unquestionably quicker. But Caleb was a big man. It would take some force to pitch him into the stream.

While the rancorous colloquy between Caleb and Ichabod continued, Asinus, aided by the noise of the storm, moved up stealthily behind Caleb. Turning his back to the man, he planted his front legs firmly, then let his rear legs fly. In less time than it takes to tell, Caleb was down in the water with Ichabod, but still Ichabod was not satisfied. The weighty Caleb had apparently landed on top of him.

While the two men remonstrated with each other in

impolite terms, Asinus again retreated into the murky gloom, confident that Jabez would soon arrive. Wherever he was, he could hardly ignore the racket his friends were now making.

Once more Asinus's hopes were quickly realized as Jabez appeared at the bank of the stream. But as Asinus prepared to give him the same treatment he had given Caleb, he began to think about the danger involved. Jabez had all those knives in his belt—and he knew how to use them. In the time it would take to blink an eye, he could put four or five daggers into you. It was almost too much to hope that you could walk up behind him, turn around and get yourself planted for a kick before he realized you were there. He was much quicker than Caleb. The sensible thing to do was to forget him, leave well enough alone and head for that hillside cave. It would be safe to go there now while the three men were occupied with one another. But Asinus savored the thought of getting the better of all three of them. He'd be taking a chance; he knew that. Yet he couldn't resist the opportunity. As he moved up carefully behind Jabez, he kept wondering how goats learned to butt. Was there a special technique for it as there was for kicking? Were you supposed to bring your head up in a hooking motion at the moment of contact? How far should you follow through? Not very far when you were at the water's edge.

He was just a few feet behind Jabez now. Lowering his head, he charged, aiming at every donkey's favorite target, the posterior.

It was not an artistic success. He brought his head up too fast and caught Jabez on the shoulder just as the man heard him coming and started to turn. Jabez, cursing, teetered for a moment, and it looked as if he might recover his balance. Asinus, alarmed at what that would mean, wondered if he should run. It was too late now. Lowering his head, he aimed again at Jabez's posterior. This time he connected precisely, dispatching the man into the turgid waters with his friends.

Asinus, braying triumphantly, trotted away to the cave in the hill. It was as cozy and comfortable as he remembered it, but he couldn't get to sleep. Not only was he flushed with the excitement of success. He was still drenched from the rain.

CHAPTER ELEVEN

THE RAIN HAD STOPPED, THE SKY HAD cleared and the first morning light was framing the mountain east of Bethel when Asinus, unable to sleep in the cave, decided it would be safe to return to the stable. He found the door still open and the other donkeys still asleep. So was the groom. If only Joseph would oversleep for a change, perhaps there might be time for a nap before beginning the day's trek to Jerusalem.

Asinus settled into his stall and had just begun to

doze when Joseph entered the stable to shatter his hope. "Well, you look comfortable," he said. "Must be nice to be a donkey. Nothing to worry about as long as you get your daily bread, as it were, and a warm stall at night." He filled Asinus's feed bin with barley, then looked around to find that no one but himself was yet up and about. "Where are our friends this morning? Must have overslept. I'll go to their room and see."

"No! Let them sleep!" Asinus cried, forgetting for the moment that Joseph couldn't understand Donkey.

Off he went to rouse Ichabod, Jabez and Caleb, leaving Asinus to hope he wouldn't find them. Was the current in that swollen stream strong enough to carry them away? No such luck, as he soon learned. Joseph returned a half hour later with his three "friends" and with Mary, ready for the day's journey.

There was murder in Ichabod's eye when he saw Asinus, apparently comfortable, in his stall. With a noticeable limp, the man walked over to the stall and said, sotto voce, "I'm not yet through with you, Mr. Donkey." Even though he and his two companions were now dry, having changed their clothes, they looked woefully bedraggled. Ichabod, in addition to whatever was wrong with his leg, seemed to be breathing with difficulty. Asinus had given his ribs some hard knocks against the wall of that building.

Mary came over to Asinus and ran a hand along his neck, then along his flanks. "You're perspiring," she said. "Are you ill? Or is it possible you're still wet from yesterday? No." She looked him in the eye. "What have you been up to, Asinus? I think you're smarter than anyone realizes. You know something about those three men, don't you? If only you could talk."

There was a loud commotion outside the stable and Phineas burst in, bellowing as usual. "You folks off to Jerusalem with me today? Cost you a shekel each. You want my protection, you gotta pay for it."

Jabez, outraged by this effrontery, shouted back at him: "What! You think we need you to protect us!"

"You need somebody," Phineas reminded him. "You can't even hold onto your purses."

Caleb said, "Maybe it was you as stole our purses."

Phineas laughed. "If I was a thief, I'd steal a purse with something in it."

Ichabod said coldly, "You'll not have a chance to steal mine, sir. We can protect ourselves."

Phineas shrugged and turned to Joseph. "Looks like it's just you and your wife, then. Two shekels. One for you and one for her, though I ought to charge extra for this troublesome donkey of yours."

"They wouldn't take your protection even if you gave it free," Ichabod said. "They're not traveling with you. They're with us."

"It didn't look like it yesterday, the way they tried to run away from you."

"That was the donkey and you know it. You said yourself he's an evil beast. You were right about that, at least."

"Yes, and I'm the only man here can handle him. He ran away from you but you notice he didn't run no more when he caught up to me."

"I thought you said he ran away when you owned him?"

"That was before he got a taste of my whip. He won't run away from me again, and this man knows it. That's why he's gonna pay to travel with me."

"He's traveling with us," Ichabod insisted. "By the time you and your starving donkeys are halfway to Jerusalem, he'll be there already."

Joseph, who had listened quietly to this argument, now said, "I don't believe you gentlemen have consulted me about any of this."

Asinus, turning toward the gentle carpenter, saw something in his face he had never seen before: anger, controlled but unmistakable. The others, however, didn't yet seem to notice it.

Ichabod said to Joseph, "Well, we all know you're not going with him. If you do, you can't go with us."

"You won't go with them if you value your life," Phineas said. "And you can't go with me unless you pay me two shekels."

With cool dignity Joseph said, "Gentlemen, I think you both misjudge me. I'll not pay for protection I have not sought. And I'll not allow anyone to tell me with whom I travel. My wife and I, and our donkey, are about to set out for Jerusalem. If any or all of you wish to accompany us, we shall welcome you. Otherwise, good day to you. I wish you well."

Asinus was astonished at Joseph's firm stand, and even more so when, a few minutes later, all the others sheepishly fell in behind him on the road. Joseph apparently had dimensions he seldom showed. But it wasn't just Joseph's strength that had made Ichabod capitulate. He was still on the trail of Joseph's money. With Phineas in the way, he might now delay his move until they reached Jerusalem, but what then? Ichabod would no doubt have new plans for them by the time they arrived there. Since he and his friends were originally from Jerusalem, they probably knew many places in the city where dark deeds could be performed.

The caravan had just passed through the gate of Bethel on the route south when Ichabod turned to Joseph. "Do you and your wife have a place to stay in Jerusalem?"

"I'm sure we'll find a place," Joseph said. "We should arrive there by midafternoon."

"I know the perfect place for you," Ichabod said. "A pleasant little inn surrounded by old olive trees, and not the least bit expensive. We'll take you to it."

Ichabod's donkey, Hepzibah, who was walking beside Asinus, said, "I wouldn't go there with him if I were you."

"I don't look forward to it," he said morosely, "but how do I turn down the invitation?"

This was the warmest, most pleasant day since they began the journey. The previous night's rain had washed the air as well as the land, making the mountains in all directions sparkle like gemstones. It was a day to live, not a day to die. But here he was trying to figure out once more how to avoid being murdered.

He was getting tired and running short of ideas. How much longer would he have to keep outwitting these cutthroats in order to survive?

His weary meditation was interrupted by the skinny roan jack in Phineas's train who had spoken to him the previous day. After waiting until Phineas went up to the front of the donkey train, the roan said to Asinus, "We got to talking about your idea last night when we were all huddled together in that rainstorm."

Asinus said, "Oh?" He didn't know what the roan was talking about.

"We all decided you were right. We're taking your advice."

"Glad to hear it," Asinus said. Why didn't this fellow leave him alone? He had something more important to do than talk to another jack donkey. He had to think of one more way to save his own life, and there wasn't much time.

"But we're not sure how to do it," the roan continued. "We thought you might give us some ideas."

"About what?"

The roan looked puzzled. "Didn't you tell me yesterday we should revolt and escape before Phineas starves us to death? We're ready."

Asinus, whose mind had been elsewhere, now looked closely at the other donkey. "Did you say you really want to escape? All of you? Are you serious?"

"If you had spent last night out in that rainstorm the way we did," the roan said, "you'd be serious, too. You haven't any idea what it was like. While you and those other three donkeys slept in your warm, dry stable . . ."

"Do you mean I've finally found some donkeys with real courage?" Asinus exclaimed. All his life he had been trying to get donkeys to revolt against the tyranny of man. He was so excited at the prospect of actually seeing it happen that he even forgot his own very acute problem for the nonce. "Now what's your plan?"

"That's what I was trying to tell you," the roan said. "We've got some ideas but we haven't settled on a plan. We were hoping you might help."

"Yes. Well, let's see. What would be the best way?"

"We could just run off into the mountains," the roan said, "but we don't know which mountains."

"You've got a problem there," Asinus admitted. "If we were farther north, in Galilee or even Samaria, it would be simple. But the mountains around here are pretty barren."

"That's what I told them," the roan said. "We're all hungry. We've got to go someplace where there's food. I suggested we wait till we get to Jerusalem."

Asinus was perplexed. "What can you do in Jerusalem?"

"As soon as we're inside the walls, one of us can give a signal and we'll scatter in all directions."

It didn't sound like a very good plan to Asinus. He was beginning to think it was easier to talk about a donkey revolt than it was to stage one. The practical aspects could be difficult. "Do you know how hard it is," he asked the roan, "for a donkey to make an independent living in a city? You've got to be a very clever thief. And even then you're sure to be caught."

"But not by Phineas," the jack said. "If we all run at the same time, he can't catch more than one of us."

"Other people will catch the rest of you."

"That wouldn't be bad, as long as it's not Phineas. In fact, I know what I'll do. I'll go to the best part of town, find a nice clean stable where the donkeys are well-fed and walk into an empty stall."

Asinus was horrified. "You do that, and the man who owns the stable will own you just as sure as Phineas owns you now."

"I don't care, as long as he feeds me."

"Do all your friends over there feel the same way?"

"Sure. We don't hate everybody. We just hate Phineas."

"People are all alike," Asinus said.

"You think so? This fellow you're with now—is he as bad as Phineas?"

"Well, no, of course not, but . . ."

"Even those other three men—they look mean, but they're not as bad as Phineas."

Hepzibah, who had been listening, broke into the conversation. "That's what you think," she said to the roan. "They're brigands and killers."

"Just the same, you look well-fed," the undernourished jack pointed out.

"It's true they make sure we get enough to eat, even if they have to steal the feed," Hepzibah admitted, "but only because they want us to be fast and strong for getaways."

"If they're that bad," the jack declared, "you three should join our revolt."

"I would," Hepzibah said, "if I thought it would work."

"I'm afraid it won't," Asinus declared pessimistically.

"Have you got any better ideas?" the jack asked.

"Not at the moment."

"Then why shouldn't we try this one?"

"Because it's not a real revolt. I can't see any sense in escaping from one owner just to be grabbed by another."

"You feel that way," Hepzibah accused him, "because your owner is good to you."

"That has nothing to do with it," Asinus insisted. "I still intend to escape. But when I do, I won't let anyone else own me. I'm heading for the far-off hills where the wild donkeys roam and where all donkeys are free. It's a paradise."

"Have you ever been there?" the jack asked.

"No, but I've heard enough about it."

"We've all heard of Paradise," the jack said, "but the world is no paradise even for people. They're always having famines and wars and revolutions."

"Yes, and they often trade one tryant for another," Asinus said. "That's exactly what you'll be doing."

"Maybe so," the jack admitted, "but we have to face the world as it is. Whatever we do, we'll still be donkeys and people will be people. They'll always use us. And even if we do end up with other tyrants, they can't be as bad as our beloved Phineas."

"You're right about that," Asinus agreed.

"Will you join us, then?"

"No, but I'll wish you luck."

For the rest of the way to Jerusalem, Asinus tried to ignore everyone else in the caravan and concentrate on his own problem, which, he decided, would become even more acute if Phineas's donkeys were going to carry out their revolt. Phineas would naturally chase after them, leaving Joseph, Mary and Asinus at the mercy of Ichabod and his cohorts. Asinus could well imagine the "pleasant little inn surrounded by old olive trees" to which Ichabod would take them. It would be, more than likely, an abandoned stable or storehouse where their corpses would lie for days before being discovered. This time everything would happen exactly according to Ichabod's plan, not only because he was more determined than ever, but also because Asinus was dead tired. He wasn't even coming up with poor ideas. His brain simply refused to function.

When the caravan of donkeys, making its way among the rough and rocky heights of Moab, came upon the first view of ancient and fabled Jerusalem, Joseph beseeched his companions to stop and contemplate its glories. Before them lay the northern wall, the hills of Moriah and Zion covered with flat-roofed houses and grand public buildings; the Garden of Gethsemane, the Mount of Olives and the Valley of Kidron to the east; Golgotha and the Valley of Jehoshaphat to the west. But dominating the whole scene, and commanding all of Joseph's reverent attention, was the great walled Temple, built by Solomon, destroyed at the time of the Captivity and now almost rebuilt, in all its splendor, by Herod.

"I shall be there by sundown for the Sabbath service," he said to Mary.

"If only women were allowed," she said wistfully.

The road became crowded as they approached the city. Outside the wall, in the shadow of the Temple, Asinus began to feel they had actually arrived as they passed through the loud and bustling stalls of the food market. Hundreds, then thousands of people swarmed around them—merchants, peddlers, beggars, other travelers, children, women with donkeys, women with water-filled vessels on their heads, women weighed down by the foods they had purchased. The odor of rotting vegetables filled the air. Chunks of meat, covered by flies, hung from great hooks in the stalls. Everywhere there were bins full of oranges, figs, pomegranates and other fruits. As was their wont at the end of each day, Joseph, Mary and their companions stopped to buy bread, fruits, wines and whatever else they would need that night and the following day. Then they pressed on to the nearest gate, prepared at last to enter the city proper.

As they passed through the huge gate and made their way into the maze of narrow streets even more crowded than the market outside the wall, Asinus began to think Phineas's donkeys had abandoned their

plan to revolt. In almost military precision they marched, one behind the other, never seeming to look right or left. They were so well behaved, in fact, he should have suspected they were awaiting a signal. The signal came, from the roan jack who had talked to Asinus, when the caravan reached a little market square that had perhaps a dozen or more streets and alleys entering it.

"Good-bye, Phineas!" the roan cried out, and suddenly the ranks broke as donkeys sprinted off in all directions, each repeating the cry, "Good-bye, Phineas!"

The raucous braying of so many donkeys at one time caught the attention of everyone within earshot, and the sight of the donkeys running pell-mell, hither and yon, put the entire square into an uproar.

The brassy voice of Phineas rose above all others. "Stop, you vermin! Get back here! Stop, I say! You infernal demons, wait till I get my hands on you!" And off he went, running at full speed after the last donkey to break ranks.

A great din of excited voices now rose up as people began grabbing at the donkeys in flight. One of the beasts, dodging outstretched hands, upset a peddler's cart. Another ran into the corner of a stall, bringing the roof down on top of it. Men were shouting, women and children screaming. Other donkeys, witnessing the excitement, decided to take part in it. Soon there were forty or fifty of them running back and forth, tipping over stalls and carts as they dodged the people trying to catch them.

Joseph and Mary watched the scene with mouths agape. So did Asinus. He was seeing at last what he had always wanted to see—a great donkey revolt. But instead of being delighted he was bewildered. Where would all these donkeys be when order was restored? Right back where they started. Most of them, anyway. Perhaps some of Phineas's donkeys would get away. He hoped so. No donkey should have to endure an owner like Phineas.

Asinus was distracted from such thoughts when he heard, above the racket, great peals of laughter behind him. He turned to find Ichabod, Jabez and Caleb beside themselves with glee.

"Look at Phineas!" Jabez squealed. "He'll never catch that beast!"

"Go, donkeys, go!" shouted Caleb.

"What a sight!" cried Ichabod. "I love it!"

By this time, the only donkeys standing still in the entire square were Asinus, Hepzibah, Aaron and Amos. Hepzibah looked at the others. "If they love it so much, let's get in it," she said, and she took off at a gallop shouting, "Good-bye, Ichabod!"

After a moment's hesitation, Amos and Aaron succumbed to the excitement and did likewise, shouting, "Good-bye, Jabez!" "Good-bye, Caleb!"

The laughter suddenly stopped. Ichabod, Jabez and Caleb, dumbfounded for a moment, took off after their donkeys in alarm, screaming deprecations at them.

Joseph, Mary and Asinus alone stood still amid the noise and confusion. Asinus was transfixed by what he was seeing. His benumbed mind couldn't comprehend it. Then, in a flash, he grasped what he should have realized long since. This donkey revolt, which he had opposed, was exactly what he needed to escape Ichabod and company.

While the uproar continued around him, he walked calmly across the square with Mary on his back and Joseph, still in apparent shock, at his heels. Choosing a street he remembered from previous trips to Jerusalem, he entered it at a stately, dignified pace, leaving the riotous scene behind him. He knew where there was a little inn on a little street a half mile away. It didn't have any olive trees, but it didn't have Ichabod, Jabez and Caleb either.

CHAPTER TWELVE

HE MORNING AFTER THE SABBATH ASI-
nus was awake so early he heard the
first chirps of birdsong; he had rested well during the
day's layover in Jerusalem. But Joseph apparently
slept late. It was two hours after dawn when he came
to the stable where he had quartered Asinus.

"I didn't really sleep," he explained to the donkey as
he adjusted Mary's saddle chair. "I feel guilty if I'm
not up and about by dawn, but I stayed in bed because
I thought Mary should sleep. She's getting very close
to her time. And I want her to be well rested this

morning. I plan to show her all the sights of Jerusalem."

Asinus was immediately alarmed. If they spent the
morning wandering around Jerusalem, Ichabod,
Jabez and Caleb were likely to find them. The city
wasn't that big, and Mary was quite conspicuous riding on his back in her chair. The safest thing to do
was to leave immediately for Bethlehem, but there
was no way Asinus could convey that to Joseph.

"Maybe we'll run into our friends again," Joseph
said, "but I suppose that's too much to hope. I'm surprised I didn't see them at the Sabbath service."

With my luck, Asinus said to himself, they'll be
waiting for us the minute we step out of this stable.

The three villains were nowhere in sight, however,
as Asinus and Joseph walked to the inn. Joseph went
to get Mary and Asinus waited in the courtyard.

It was an hour or more before Joseph emerged from
the inn and when he did he looked disappointed.
"Mary doesn't want to see the sights of Jerusalem," he
announced. "I don't know why. It's not like her. She's
usually full of life and ready to go."

Asinus let out a sigh of relief. Mary obviously knew
what she was doing. She was no more eager than he
was to run into that trio of villains. She couldn't possibly know the depths of their depravity or the partic-
ulars of their evil schemes, but she knew enough not
to trust them. Why couldn't Joseph see through them?
Was it because he was so good himself he couldn't
conceive of anyone else being bad? Or was it because,
as Asinus had to acknowledge when he stopped to

think of it, the three villains hadn't yet committed any villainy against Joseph? How long could they be prevented from doing so? Their frustrations had made them more vicious and determined than ever, as did the additional money now in Joseph's purse. They fairly drooled each time he showed it to them. It would be foolish to think they were not lying in wait someplace, perhaps at the city gate on the road to Bethlehem.

When Mary finally emerged from the inn about midday she was apparently in pain, yet she didn't mention it as Joseph helped her into her saddle chair on Asinus's back. "I hope you got some rest," she said to Asinus, patting his mane affectionately.

As they walked through the busy city toward the Bethlehem-Hebron road, Asinus expected at any moment to hear the fulsome voice of Ichabod calling out to them in his unctuous tones. But they passed through the western gate and headed south and he began to think they might actually have succeeded in losing Joseph's three "friends." It was another pleasant, sunny day. Walking along a path which paralleled Jerusalem's west wall and skirted Mount Zion, Asinus began to feel carefree, then almost euphoric. It puzzled him. Why should he feel this good? Was it simply because for the first time in several days he didn't have to face the possibility of sudden death? That was a relief, to be sure, but it didn't change the fact that he was still a chattel of this man who walked beside him. It didn't change the fact that for seven days now he had been doing what he had promised himself never to do—allowing human beings to use him as a beast of burden. After all this time on the road, he hadn't yet fulfilled his plans to escape. Why not? He could honestly say he hadn't had a decent opportunity until the third night out, after Joseph's pocket had been picked in Shechem, but it would have been too human to leave Joseph and Mary when they were destitute. Then he had fallen asleep the fourth night after recovering Joseph's purse. He couldn't help that. He was exhausted. And the fifth night he spent running for his life through the streets of Bethel in that awesome storm. He might have been able to sneak out the city gate after dumping Ichabod, Jabez and Caleb into the water, but again he was exhausted after the chase, and the storm was still raging. He might also have made a run for it during that riotous donkey revolt in Jerusalem, but he had Mary on his back at the time, besides which there was no place to go in Jerusalem. There was no place to go even outside Jerusalem. The hills around here were parched. There wasn't enough grass to feed a goat. He'd have to wait now until the return trip north, and then escape. There was really no hurry. Maybe that was why he felt so good today. There was no pressure on him.

They stopped twice at wells along the way because Mary was uncommonly thirsty. She was moving more slowly than usual and Asinus felt sure she was in pain.

"We must get some swaddling bands," she said to Joseph during one of their stops. "We'll also need some soft cotton cloth and a few other things."

"We can get everything you need in Bethlehem," he assured her.

She smiled at him and put a hand on his chin. "Will you forgive me?"

"For what?"

"I know how much you wanted to see Jerusalem," she said. "Perhaps we can stop awhile on the way back, but this morning I just wasn't up to it."

"I can well imagine. I shouldn't even have expected it of you."

"Are you excited about going to Bethlehem?" she asked. "The home of your ancestors. Wasn't it in these very hills that David hid when King Saul came looking for him?"

"Indeed, my dear. We pass near David's Well, I believe, before we reach the city. I can hardly wait to see it."

As they walked south, the soil, while still rocky, seemed to be more fertile, and there was enough grass on the hillsides to support sheep. Asinus saw several flocks, at intervals, and now and then he would see groups of shepherds watching them. Soon he was able to see the familiar walls of Bethlehem in the distance, and its limestone houses, like white cubes climbing the hillside. They missed David's Well, near the fork in the road leading to Hebron, but they did see Rachel's Tomb, and Joseph told Mary the story of Benoni, which, of course, she already knew.

They were only a few hundred cubits from the Bethlehem city gate, an hour or so before the winter sunset, when Asinus's cheerful mood was shattered by the sight of Ichabod, Jabez and Caleb, with their donkeys, standing at the side of the road ahead.

Joseph, seeing them, waved and called out to them. All three returned his wave, then came to meet him with friendly greetings.

"God is good," Joseph said. "Once again I thought we had lost you, but once again He has restored us to one another."

"We were determined to find you," Ichabod said, "and it wasn't that difficult. We knew you were coming to Bethlehem. It was only a matter of waiting for you."

"But I thought you three had intended to come only as far as Jerusalem," Joseph said.

"We changed our plans," Ichabod explained, "and I'm happy we did. Otherwise we might have missed you. How did you fare in that diabolical revolt of the donkeys? I see you still have your great white beast."

"Asinus? Oh indeed. He never once lost his poise during the whole affair. He walked right through it as stately as you please."

"I can't say as much for these three brutes of ours," Ichabod said, "but I think I can promise they'll never lose their heads and take part in another donkey riot. We try to be kind, but once in a while we have to be firm."

Asinus turned to Aaron, Amos and Hepzibah. "What did these cruel monsters do to you?"

"Please," Hepzibah said in painful tones, "don't ask."

"One reason we came looking for you," Ichabod explained to Joseph, "is that we have a place for you to stay. A quaint little inn surrounded by terebinth trees, and not the least bit expensive. We'll take you to it directly. Your wife is tired, I'm sure."

So it's terebinth trees this time, Asinus said to himself. In Jerusalem it was old olive trees.

Mary said to Joseph, "Don't you think we should find a place ourselves? We don't want to impose on these gentlemen."

"It's no imposition at all," Ichabod assured her. "We're staying there ourselves and I've already told our host you'd be coming."

"It might seem impolite," Joseph said to Mary, "if we were to reject such a friendly gesture."

Ichabod reached for Asinus's headstall and said, "Here, I'll lead your donkey."

"That's not necessary," Joseph said. "Just show us the way."

As they walked through the Bethlehem gate, Joseph said to Mary, "I'm glad we're here at last. You look tired, my dear. If only I lived in the city of my ancestors, like most people, you wouldn't have had to travel like this, and in the middle of winter, just so I could pay my taxes. But then, on the other hand, if I lived here in Bethlehem, I might never have met you."

"Before we go anyplace," Mary said to Joseph, "don't you think we'd better get the things I'll be needing?"

"I haven't forgotten," Joseph said to her. And to Ichabod, "We have to stop first in a marketplace and it may take a while. I don't want to delay you gentlemen. Why don't you tell us the way to the inn and we'll meet you there."

"Nothing of the kind," Ichabod insisted. "We'll take you to the marketplace and wait for you. That's all there is to it. We'll hear no argument."

It was a sizable market street to which he led them, with a variety of shops and stalls, but almost deserted since the hour was late. Ichabod, Jabez and Caleb tethered their donkeys outside a tool shop, across the street from a wineshop, to which they repaired as soon as Joseph and Mary disappeared into a nearby cloth shop.

Asinus, untethered as usual, waited with Amos, Aaron and Hepzibah. "Tell me about his 'quaint little inn' with terebinth trees," he said. "What is it, actually?"

Amos said, "It's an abandoned stable at the far end of town."

"And we don't have to tell you," Aaron added, "what will happen to all three of you if you go there."

"Where is it? On the road to Tekoa?"

"Yes, how did you know?"

"I lived here when Phineas owned me. When I ran away from him I got to know this town pretty well."

Hepzibah said, "I hope you're ready to run away again."

"I would," Asinus said, "but it doesn't seem to work with Ichabod, Jabez and Caleb. I've already run away from them three times and they've caught up every time. I've got to get rid of them for good." His mind turned to a new train of thought. On a front table in the open shop outside which the donkeys were standing was an impressive display of tools—axes, saws, hatchets, knives, sickles and hammers. He knew how expensive such tools were. He looked at Amos, Aaron and Hepzibah. Each of them was carrying two bulky packs.

"I've got an idea that might work," Asinus said. "And you three don't have to do anything but stand still. Will you let me try it?"

"As long as they don't beat us again," Hepzibah said. "They were brutal when they caught us in Jerusalem."

"Don't worry, they won't blame you," Asinus said. "Just stand where you are."

He peered into the shop and saw that the proprietor was busy with a customer at the rear. What he had in mind should be easy in one regard. Donkeys weren't expected to be thieves. Shopkeepers paid little or no attention to them. But it would be difficult in another regard. Donkeys, like other animals, never get any practice at picking up tools. Indeed, human beings were always bragging that they, alone, could handle tools, that no other animals could use them. He'd soon show them how wrong they were about that. Or at least he'd try. Lacking hands, he'd have to make do with his mouth.

After another glance at the preoccupied shopkeeper, he clamped his teeth onto the nearest tool on the table, a long-handled ax. Satisfied that he had a firm hold, he picked it up and tucked it into the crease between the two packs on Hepzibah's back. Then he took a saw, being careful not to cut his mouth on its jagged teeth, and tucked it in between the packs on Aaron's back. One by one, he picked up more axes and saws, hammers, hatchets, sickles and knives from the table. As quickly as possible, he nestled each of these tools into the space between the packs on all three donkeys, making sure the handles stuck out visibly in the rear.

"When those three come out of the wineshop," he said to the donkeys, "try to turn facing them so they won't see the tools sticking out in back."

A few minutes later the wineshop door opened and the men emerged, looking tipsy. All three swayed slightly as they ambled into the street.

Jabez, glancing toward the cloth shop where Joseph had taken Mary, said, "Where's that rich carpenter?"

Caleb said, "He hadn't better spend too much of our money on swaddling clothes."

Ichabod, who seemed as angry as he was inebriated, said, "They'd better come out soon. This thing has dragged on too long."

Asinus, watching them, prepared to put his tool plan into action against them, but it would work better, he decided, if he were to launch it the minute they took hold of their donkeys. Unfortunately, they were ignoring their donkeys. They remained in the middle of the street, cursing Joseph as their impatience increased.

"We should've been rid of these people and their infernal donkey five days ago," Ichabod declared, with a snarling tone in his voice. "This time we finish the job, and no more delays. You hear? I'm not letting them slip away again."

Finally Joseph and Mary emerged from the cloth shop, laden with bundles, and walked down the deserted, semidarkened street toward them. As Joseph approached, he said apologetically, "I'm sorry we've kept you waiting. I want to thank you for your company and your kind offer to take us to your inn, but we've decided to decline. My wife's time is almost upon her. She prefers an inn where we can be alone."

Ichabod, at this announcement, looked stricken. He could no longer conceal his fury. "Who cares what she prefers?" he exclaimed. "She's only a woman. Are you not in charge of your own household?"

Joseph drew himself up in amazement at this outburst. "I hope I heard you wrong, sir. 'Only a woman'?"

Ichabod, angry and in his cups, had lost his usual self-control. "She and that donkey have been leading you by the nose ever since we began this journey. But no more. You're coming with us. We know just the place for you."

As Ichabod moved toward him, Joseph stared in amazement, unable to believe the man was serious.

"I'll grab her," Ichabod cried out to Jabez and Caleb. "You two grab him."

At the realization that Mary was actually threatened, Joseph sprang into action. Dropping his bundles and sweeping her into his arms, he deposited her at the mouth of a narrow alley between two buildings. Then he turned, blocking the alley entrance, to face the three men. "You may do your worst against me," he declared, "but you will not touch this woman."

Though they were upon him in an instant, they soon found they had their hands full against him. As the struggle began, he proved stronger than any single one of them. And he used the alley walls cleverly to prevent them from flanking him. Nevertheless, Ichabod soon got hold of his legs and the other two seemed about to overpower him when Asinus, though handicapped by the chair and the packs on his back, came crashing into them, knocking them aside. Before these two could recover, he began stomping on Ichabod's back, quickly persuading him to let go of Joseph and scramble to safety.

Cursing the donkey, who now stood beside Joseph in the mouth of the alley, the three men regrouped and reassessed the situation. Though a frontal attack no longer looked promising, Ichabod saw a solution.

"Go around the block," he ordered Jabez, "and come up the alley behind the woman. With your dagger at her throat, he'll soon give up."

Asinus decided Ichabod was right. There was no way he and Joseph could protect Mary from Jabez's dagger. And once Jabez got hold of her they could threaten to kill her on the spot if Joseph refused to surrender. There was not a moment to spare. Asinus thought of the tools he had stashed between the back packs of Hepzibah, Amos and Aaron, all three of whom stood watching the struggle.

Bolting from the alley, Asinus ran to the front of the tool shop, where he raised a rear hoof, lifted the now half-empty table into the air, and brought it down on its side with a great clatter.

At this unexpected development, Ichabod and Caleb, who were again closing in on Joseph, glanced toward the tool shop. But before they had time to grasp the situation, the tool-shop proprietor, aroused by the noise of the falling table, appeared with a lamp and saw the depleted pile of his merchandise strewn upon the ground.

"My tools!" he cried. "My tools!"

Looking up, he noticed the three donkeys in front of the shop, all with several tools sticking out between their packs.

"Who owns these donkeys?" the shopkeeper demanded.

Ichabod, suspecting nothing, said, "We do, sir. Those are our donkeys."

"Guards!" the shopkeeper shouted. "Guards! Guards! Call the Guards!"

The whole street was suddenly in an uproar as several people, including three town Guards, rushed to the scene.

"There they are!" the shopkeeper screamed, pointing at Ichabod and Caleb, who stood bewildered. In a matter of moments, the shopkeeper had pulled all the tools out from between the packs on the donkeys' backs.

"There's been a mistake!" Ichabod protested when he realized he was being accused.

"There sure has," one of the Guards agreed, "and it was you that made it."

"We been framed!" Caleb cried.

Joseph, now that Ichabod and Caleb were no longer menacing him, brought Mary forth from the alley, holding her in his arms.

A moment later, Jabez emerged from the alley, pursuing them with dagger in hand. When he saw the crowd, he quickly put away the dagger and went over to Ichabod.

"What's going on now?" he asked.

Ichabod pointed at the shopkeeper. "He says we stole some tools from him."

"We didn't do nothing of the kind," Jabez declared.

"Of course not," said the Guard, with a derisive smile. He pointed to Asinus. "I guess that donkey loaded all this stuff on your donkeys' backs."

Ichabod glanced balefully at Asinus, then cast a heavy sigh in apparent resignation. "I wouldn't be a bit surprised," he said.

Mary, looking pale and breathing heavily, said, "Joseph, I'm proud of you and I'm proud of Asinus."

"Yes, it was Asinus who saved us," Joseph declared. "How could I have misjudged those men so completely when our donkey saw through them from the start? I'm afraid Ichabod was right about one thing. Asinus really has been leading me by the nose." He paused, then broke into a wide smile. "Thank God for that."

Though Mary also smiled, she could not conceal a clouded expression that crossed her face at the same time.

Joseph, noticing it, looked closely at her. "Mary!" he cried, "are you . . ."

"I'm afraid we'd better find an inn as soon as possible," she said.

But Joseph, a stranger in Bethlehem, knew nothing of the inns there. Asinus, who was familiar with the town, tried to remember the location of the nearest one. It seemed to him there was a decent little place about three blocks away. As soon as Mary was back in her saddle chair, he took off up the street in search of it, with Joseph running along behind him. Full darkness had set in by the time they stopped in front of the place Asinus had in mind.

Joseph, recognizing it as an inn, exclaimed, "Asinus! You've done it again. How did we ever get along without you?" Before rushing inside, he threw his arms around the donkey and gave him a great hug.

When he emerged from the inn, Joseph had a worried look on his face. "There's no room here," he said.

Asinus could now hear Mary's breathing. She sat restlessly upon his back. Again he took off without delay, hurrying along the same street to another inn he remembered having seen. Alas, there was no room at this one either, as Joseph soon learned. In quick succession, Asinus took them to two more inns, but with the same result.

"Are you all right?" Joseph asked Mary.

"Yes, dear, I'm fine," she said, "but I don't think I have much more time."

Asinus, unfortunately, had now exhausted his knowledge of Bethlehem's lodging houses. Yet he had to take this woman someplace, and soon. Where, oh where? The only places that came to mind were several abandoned stables at the southern edge of town, on the way to Tekoa. He had hidden in one of those stables when he was trying to escape from Phineas. It was a sturdy enough building with thick walls, plenty of straw and a well behind it. Not bad. Hardly fancy but fairly cozy, at least by donkey standards. Would Joseph and Mary consider it acceptable? Human beings could be finicky at times.

Afraid to run because of Mary's increasingly critical condition, Asinus, in the semidarkness, walked through town to the Tekoa road as fast as his legs would carry him. The stable he had in mind was still there. He wondered if it might be the one to which Ichabod had planned to bring them. The door was ajar. Putting his nose against it, he pushed it open and entered, with Mary still on his back and Joseph right behind them. It was pitch-black inside, but Joseph was able to light an oil lamp he carried in one of the packs on Asinus's back.

"It looks clean," Joseph said to Mary. "Here, let me help you down. It's not cold tonight, and there's plenty of straw. I can make a bed for you in that corner."

He helped her to the corner where she sat on a stool while he fashioned a good thick mattress of straw and spread his own cloak on top of it. As soon as she was stretched out upon it, he said, "Now, if only I could find some water."

Asinus stamped his left foot for attention and then started toward the door.

"You'd better follow him," Mary said. "He seems to know where everything is."

Asinus lead Joseph to the well, where Joseph filled three skins with water. When they returned to the stable, Mary was already in labor. Joseph rushed to her aid while Asinus stood at a distance.

Within a remarkably short time, he heard the sound of a baby crying.

"It's a boy!" Joseph shouted. "It's a boy!"

"You knew it would be," Mary answered, in a voice tired but still strong.

"He's beautiful!" Joseph cried. "Look at him! Hold him!"

Taking the baby in her arms, she wrapped him in the swaddling clothes she had just bought. "Yes, dear," she said. "He's more than beautiful."

Joseph fell to his knees. "I feel so small," he said. "I don't know what to say." Stretching out his arms in prayer, he cried, "Thank you! Thank you! Thank you!" as if his God were right in front of him. Asinus could scarcely believe the aura of happiness which seemed to surround the man.

Getting to his feet, Joseph crawled onto the straw bed, encompassing mother and child in his arms. Then he pulled back. Both he and Mary looked down, with tears of joy, at the little bundle.

"Asinus!" Joseph called out. "Where are you? Come see our child!"

Asinus felt almost timid as he walked over to them. He had never before seen human beings act like this. He had never dreamed that people could be capable of such feeling. Both Joseph and Mary looked up at him and smiled. Even the baby smiled.

"Wait!" Joseph said, and, leaving the bed, he went to one of the two packs Asinus had carried all the way from Nazareth. After rummaging around inside it, he pulled out a sack, which he opened. It was the sugar, lumpy now, that he had bought before leaving home. Choosing the biggest lump he could find, he offered it as a gift for Asinus.

The donkey took the sugar in his mouth, savored it, then rubbed against Joseph's shoulder to show his thanks. Though it was only a lump of sugar, it filled him with a rush of gratitude he had never before experienced. He wondered why he had ever been impatient with Joseph, why he had ever thought the man stupid or crazy. He wasn't stupid. He simply looked at things differently from other people. Maybe it was the other people who were stupid.

Turning to Mary, Asinus gazed at her for a long time, transfixed by the beatific smile on her face. Joseph was fortunate to have such a wife. But she was fortunate to have him, too. They were made for each

other. Mary smiled at the infant, then at Joseph, then at the infant again. She wrapped his swaddling clothes more tightly around him. Asinus lowered his eyes to the child and once again found himself transfixed. He had always hated children, but he couldn't bring himself to hate this one. For several minutes he gazed down at him, puzzled by his own feelings. Finally, he said to himself, That's a really good-looking baby. When he's old enough, I'll teach him to ride.